PROTECT YOUR MONEY

A STORY ABOUT STOCKBROKERS

WES CRAWFORD

iUniverse, Inc.
Bloomington

Protect Your Money
A Story about Stockbrokers

iUniverse books may be ordered through booksellers or by contacting:

iUniverse
1663 Liberty Drive
Bloomington, IN 47403
www.iuniverse.com
1-800-Authors (1-800-288-4677)

ISBN: 978-1-4697-5816-9 (sc)
ISBN: 978-1-4697-5815-2 (e)

Printed in the United States of America

iUniverse rev. date: 03/29/2012

To my wife, Marlyn and daughter, Angie; two lovely and beautiful ladies, and to my friend and team-mate, Mickey Johnson; the toughest man I know

CHAPTER 1

They will be trained to deceive the public, but they do not know it yet. They were in their first day of training at one of the Dallas branches of Damon, Witz, and Rabin, a major Wall Street brokerage firm. The firm was referred to on the street as Damon. The trainees will spend sixty days preparing for the NASD Series Seven test, which is required to become a stockbroker. They will then go to New York for further training and indoctrination. After that, they will be unleashed upon the public.

There were four of them. Their names were John Simpson, Joe Dunigan, Bob Reynoso, and Ted Miller. Before opting to become a stockbroker, John, the oldest at 45, was a successful business executive. When he looked at the youth of the other trainees, he wonders if he made the right decision when he changed careers. Joe was a burned out commodities trader. He was a sharp dresser and wore expensive suits. Bob was a minister. He was offended by the profanity used by most of the brokers he has encountered. Ted was fresh out of college. He was full of enthusiasm and hope.

They would be located in a large conference room and would sit at a large table, which was against a wall. They were close together so they could help each other if necessary.

The morning of the first day brought a pep talk and lecture by the Branch Manager, Mike Rabinovitz. He was a very small man and obviously had a Napoleon complex. He strutted around like a peacock. He started the session by attempting to intimidate everyone. He told them that most

1

of them would not be here six months from now unless they did exactly as he said. He said they were not financial advisors. They were salesmen. The object of the game was to generate commissions. Commissions made the firm happy and their family happy. He said they must keep the phone glued to their ear. That was the way leads were created. The more leads the better because if you threw enough shit against the wall, some of it stuck. Also, they had better make certain that they passed the Series Seven. If they failed it, they would be terminated. They would not get a second chance. He asked if there were any questions.

"Why can't we give advice?" John asked.

"You can, but be certain it's incorporated into a sales pitch and close the sale. Remember that the mission is to generate commissions," Mike replied.

"That doesn't appear entirely ethical."

"What's ethical? To me, ethical is taking care of your family and the firm by generating commissions."

"Why can't you get business by advising them and winning their trust?" Bob queried.

"It's possible, but your closing rate will be extremely low. Instead, come across as an expert and tell them that the investment you're pitching is the ideal one for them."

"Mike, what you've said makes sense to me. I'm looking forward to working for you," Joe intoned.

"With that attitude, you'll be very successful in this business. Don't lose your enthusiasm."

Ted was intimidated and stayed silent.

Mike then passed out the study guides and practice tests. He then informed the group that the practice tests are taken from the real test. These multiple-choice tests were scratch offs to keep one from changing their answer. He then instructed the trainees to give their daily tests to his secretary. The scores would be posted outside Mike's office.

After Mike left, a lively discussion ensued. The talk centered on what is ethical and their opinion of Mike.

"Mike's philosophy is wrong. I think we should try to help clients, not take advantage of them," Bob said.

"I agree with you. If you win their trust, they'll be clients forever. The commissions will follow," John said

"I can't stomach his hard sell approach. You'll piss off more people than you sell," Ted added.

"You guys are all full of it. The way to win at this game is to put a hard close on them and get your commission. If the investment doesn't work out, find another sucker," Joe stated.

"You sound like a crooked used car salesman," John said.

"Joe, what you said is not only unethical, but also immoral," Bob added.

"Preacher, don't give me a sermon. The only thing I'm interested in is money. I'll make more of it than all of you combined," Joe replied.

The conversation was interrupted when Mike came in to pass out some propaganda supporting his philosophy. He quickly left.

"Does anyone except me think Mike is a jerk?" Ted asked.

"He's my kind of man. If we listen to him, we'll be very successful in this business." Joe replied.

"If we listen to him we're likely to lose our license," John noted.

"I don't think he cares about either the client or his employees," Bob said.

"You people are missing the point. It's all about money. You can milk the clients out of a lot of their money. What's wrong with that?" Joe said.

"You're sick," John replied.

"What you're saying is not only unethical, it's immoral," Bob said."

"Let's talk about something else. Joe's attitude is making me feel ill." Ted said

That comment got a good laugh, including one from Joe.

After that, everyone turned to his or her study guides. The rest of the week was spent studying and taking daily tests, with limited conversation.

Everyone was getting serious about passing the test. John, who has an MBA, comprehended the material easily. He was the appointed tutor for the group. Bob was picking things up readily. Joe, and especially Ted, was struggling. John spent as much time with them as he could spare.

During the second week, everybody was more relaxed because they knew each other better. On Monday, Ted walked in with a smile on his face.

"What are you so happy about?" John asked.

"Because I have a date with head knocker tonight," Ted relied.

This drew a laugh from everyone.

"Who in the hell is head knocker?" Joe inquired.

"I met her in college. I didn't know she was in Dallas until yesterday. We call her head knocker because she loves to bang her head against the wall while having sex. It's really wild," Ted answered.

"You should have your head knocked for going out with her," Bob said.

"It sounds somewhat exotic, but I wouldn't touch it. She could become brain damaged like you are" John said

"You guys don't appreciate a good time," Ted replied.

After that weird exchange, they began studying. John and Bob were posting good grades on their daily exams. Joe and Ted were not doing well.

Mike walked into the room.

"Some of you trainees aren't doing worth a flip on your daily exams. You know who you are. Come to my office immediately," Mike said.

Mike left and Joe and Ted followed him to his office.

They entered Mike's office sheepishly.

What the hell are you trying to do? End your career before it starts? You're both making in the sixties and low seventies on your exams. That doesn't cut it. Until your scores are in the eighties, I want you to stay an hour after work for extra study time. Is there a problem with that?" Mike asked.

Both replied no and left.

Joe and Ted entered the training room.

"What happened?" Bob asked.

"We got our butts reamed because of our low scores," Joe replied.

"Yeah, it was bad. We have to stay an extra hour after work until we get our scores in the eighties," Ted said

John and Bob agreed to help them get their scores up. John and Bob were both scoring in the nineties. They were also finishing their tests by two or three in the afternoon; so they had time to help the other two. Bob wanted to tutor Ted. As a result, John inherited Joe. The remainder of the second week was devoted to John and Bob finishing their work and helping the other two.

By the middle of the third week, both Joe and Ted were making progress. Joe's scores were in the mid to high seventies. He was catching on. Ted's were in the low seventies. This was an improvement from the sixties. However, it put him at risk to fail the Series Seven.

Mike came in.

"Joe, I want to see you outside," Mike said.

Joe went outside.

"I want to compliment you on your improvement in scores. Keep improving. I like your attitude about maximizing commissions. I have big plans for you," Mike said.

"I appreciate your confidence in me. I'll not let you down. I enjoy working for you and I'm looking forward to a long relationship. My goal is to be your best broker," Joe stated.

"You're a good man. Tell Ted to come to my office."

Joe entered the training room and told Ted to go to Mike's office.

"What's the deal?" Ted asked.

"I don't know. He didn't tell me," Joe replied.

Ted left and entered Mike's office.

"Ted, we have a problem," Mike said.

"What is it?" Ted said.

"You're scoring in the low seventies on your exams and you're almost half way through your test preparation. If you get a little nervous during the test, you'll flunk it. What the hell did they teach you in college? Did they teach you how to study? You're finance major. Didn't they teach you anything about the stock market? You need to get your act together or you will not make it. Do have anything to say?"

"I'll try to do better."

"OK, get back to studying."

Ted came back to the training room with his head down. Everyone noticed and did not comment. John told a joke in an attempt to break the ice. Everybody laughed except Ted. There was a long period of silence. Finally, John gets up and motioned Ted outside.

"I think we should go to the deli downstairs and talk," John said.

"Let's go," Ted said.

They took the elevator twenty floors down and walked into the deli. They ordered soft drinks and nachos.

"You look like you're having a bad day," John said.

"A bad three weeks is more like it," Ted replied.

"Everyone faces adversity sometime in their life. How you handle that determines your success. You're facing it at an early age. That's good because it will prepare you for the future. Don't give up. You're too young for that."

"What should I do?"

"If you're not giving a hundred percent, do it. If you give it and you fail, you have nothing to be ashamed of because you've given all you have. I had a successful business career, but I was fired twice. If I had given up, I probably would be a pauper. Ted, how do you feel about our conversation? Do have any comments?"

"What you've said makes sense to me. I feel better about the entire situation."

"Let's finish our nachos."

While snacking, John learned that Ted was an all conference football player in college. Also, due to constraints on his time, he barely graduated. In addition, he is currently involved in working with underprivileged children. Furthermore, he volunteered time to deliver food for the Meals On Wheels program. John thinks to himself that Ted is a special person. John told him that regardless of what happens with this job, he would be a success in life. Ted expressed his appreciation for the comment.

By this time, they had finished their nachos and drinks; so they went to the elevator and returned to the training room.

They entered the room. Joe says,

"What the hell was that all about?" Joe asked.

"Actually, it's none of your business," John replied.

"Right, it's none of your damn business," Ted added.

"It'll be my business when I'm making tons of money and you guys want to know how I'm doing it," Joe said.

"I don't think I want to know," Bob replied.

"That sums it up," Ted said.

"Let's cut out the crap," John said. "We're a team. We need to stick together. Let's get back to work."

"I'm sorry about that, Joe," Ted said. "I'm having a rough trip. I don't need to take it out on everybody else."

"That's OK," Joe replies. "It takes a real man to apologize."

The fourth week was hectic. Not only are the trainees required to do their studying and tests, but also to attend meetings explaining the firm's array of products. This mixture did not include stocks and bonds. Instead, it encompassed high commission products such as real estate partnerships, managed commodity accounts, and some really exotic and high risk investments. The product presentations ended at mid morning on Thursday.

The trainees returned to the training room.

"What did you think about the products?" Bob asked.

"Almost all of them are high risk. I'd rather put them in a good stock or mutual fund. At least, they'll have an excellent chance with these." John replied.

"I want to recommend conservative investments. That enables you to keep their business." Ted said.

"I can't believe what I'm hearing. Generating commissions is the name of the game. If the investment doesn't work out, get another client." Joe said.

"I want to treat my clients right. They deserve that much. I'll not put them in unsuitable investments because of the commission rate. Who knows? Maybe I'll fail at this business. But I'll go home each day with a clear conscience." John replied.

"You're missing the boat. You'll come around." Joe said.

"We're half way through our test preparation. We need to study." Bob said.

Friday was also spent studying, with almost no conversation.

By the middle of the fifth week, Joe had his scores in the eighties; so he was out of Mike's punishment program. Ted continued to have problems and remained in the doghouse.

John asked Bob to have lunch with him. They went to El Chico, which serves Mexican food, a staple of the Texas diet.

"What's the deal with Ted?" John inquired.

"He doesn't get it. I've tried everything. For some reason, he's having difficulty remembering what he's studied. He's not dumb. I think he's either nervous or intimidated. But I don't know what to do about it." John replied.

"That's a shame because he's doing a lot of good things in his personal life."

"Yeah, he's told me about them."

"How do you feel about the brokerage business so far?"

"I don't know enough about it yet to reach a valid conclusion. However, I have concluded that working with Mike will be difficult. It's his way or no way."

"I feel about the same way. Maybe Mike will loosen up when we're producing."

"I doubt it."

They paid their tab and returned to the office.

As they entered the training room, Mike walked in.

"Where have you two been?" Mike asked

"At lunch," John replied."

"From now on, bring your lunch. You need to be studying."

"We're not children."

"If you want to work here, you'll do as I say."

"As a result of this conversation, I'm no longer certain that I want to work here."

"John, let's go to my office and discuss this."

They left for Mike's office.

"Maybe I was a bit too harsh. What do you think?" Mike said.

"I believe that you are probably correct. Bob and I are mature adults. We shouldn't be treated like high school students." John said

"Let's do this. I'll back off. I'm certain that you'll be a good broker. I need good brokers because of the high turnover in this business. Is this OK with you?"

"That'll work."

They shook hands and John returned to the training room.

"What happened?" Joe asked.

"I'm still here." John replied.

"You're screwing up, John."

"No, I'm only defending my principles."

"You're principles will not buy you a cup of coffee."

"No, but I have peace with myself. How about you?"

"This whole conversation is a bunch of bullshit. You sound like some philosopher. Philosophers starve to death."

"Maybe so. But I'd rather go hungry than screw someone out of their hard earned money."

"What difference does it make? If we don't get it, somebody else will. Can't you comprehend that?"

"No. If another broker is unethical, that doesn't mean that I must emulate him."

"You're a good guy, but you'll never make it in this business."

"We'll see who makes it."

At the beginning of the sixth week, the group was dead serious about their studying because they take the Series Seven a week from the coming Saturday. Conversation was limited to questions about the study material.

The seventh week was even more intense. They all will go to SMU on Saturday and take the test. It will take four to five hours to complete it. It is a grueling test. By the middle of the morning Friday, everyone is burned out and they decided to go home and rest for the test.

The last week was spent waiting for the test results, which would come out on Friday. In the meantime, Mike gave them handouts on the products of the firm. They were all looking forward to going to New York. John was the only one that has been there.

"What's it like?" Bob asked.

"You must experience it to know. It's a unique city and it's very multicultural. There are thousands of interesting things there," John replied.

"Would you live there?"

"Probably not. I'm an outdoors person and require more space than is available there."

They will leave for New York on Sunday.

On Friday, the test results arrived. Mike walked in and said that he wants to see the trainees individually in his office. They all passed except Ted. Mike fired him.

Back in the training room, everybody wished Ted good luck. He said that he enjoyed his relationship with them and wished them good luck. He then turned and left the room. There were no comments.

CHAPTER 2

They arrived in New York on Sunday afternoon and took one of the famous New York taxis to the hotel. Joe and Bob were somewhat concerned about the driver's skills, his constant use of the horn, and his propensity to show his middle finger to other drivers. John welcomed them to New York. The hotel was across the street from Grand Central Station, which made it convenient for a subway trip to the office building where they will go each day for training.

They checked in. They had roommates. John drew one from Chicago. Joe got one from Baltimore, and Bob was assigned a Fort Worth guy. Joe, the only single one, commented that he should have a female roommate. John informed him that he probably was not good enough to score with her. Joe laughed and related that it would be fun trying.

They got to their rooms. Though it was an older hotel, the accommodations were not bad. They were spacious and there were two double beds. In addition, there was a kitchen, complete with a refrigerator, stove, sink, cooking utensils, plates, and silverware. It was more like an apartment than a hotel room. The closets were more than adequate.

There were trainees from three other firms in residence at the facility; so they will be able to compare notes.

In the evening, the Damon group went to an Irish pub, Gallagher's. It was just around the corner. Previous trainees recommended it. As they entered the pub, the bar was to the left. The buffet was to the right. When they walked past the bar, a large room in the back had twenty or thirty regular tables and one very long table. The beer was reasonable and the food in the buffet, for $6.95, was great. This was cheap fare for the Big Apple. They decided to make this their regular hang out. The place was full of trainees from other firms. Apparently, the word was out about Gallagher's. Everybody mingled and made new friends. Most of them were enthusiastic and believed that they had great futures in the brokerage business. Many of them will be disappointed.

The next morning, all of the trainees boarded the subway car bound for the building where the Training Center was located. The car pulled into the building and they entered the lobby. The lobby was huge. There are numerous business establishments in the lobby, including newsstands, restaurants and bars.

"Why are they drinking this early?" Bob asked.

"Apparently, they're loosening up for the day ahead," John replied.

"Anything goes in this city."

"I believe it."

"You haven't seen anything yet."

"I'm not sure I want to."

"You don't have a choice. You'll see it."

"I'm not sure I'm comfortable in this damn city," Joe said. "It's too big and too crowded."

"You'll adapt to it," John said.

They approached the elevator and went upstairs to the training room. It was a large room with long tables and chairs behind them. There were three aisles. One was in the center of the room and two were on each side of the room. There were 71 trainees from all areas of the country. It was a diverse group. There were several minorities and approximately a third of the group was female. This day was spent handing out materials, reviewing some of them, and pep talks from not only members of management but also local brokers. The entire session was a waste of time.

They boarded the subway and returned to the hotel. While they were walking from the subway to the hotel, a street person was urinating on the sidewalk.

"What the hell is this?" Joe asked.

"I presume that he had an urge," John answered.

"John, you were right. I'm convinced now that I haven't seen it all," Bob said.

"Why don't the cops do something about that?" Joe asked.

"They have bigger fish to fry in this city. They would need to triple the police force to arrest street people. Then what do they do with them? It's not cost effective or practical." John answered.

"Dallas is looking better and better," Bob said.

"Yeah, and the people here are aloof and unfriendly," Joe added.

"You guys have only been here two days. The culture here is much different than Dallas. You're experiencing culture shock. The people here aren't really unfriendly. Once you gain their confidence and become friends, you'll find that they are some of the finest people you've met. They're vibrant and giving, just like the people in Dallas. The difference is that they are not friendly to strangers the way we are," John said

"You're giving us a lesson," Bob said.

As they entered the hotel, they agreed to meet at Gallagher's at seven o'clock for a beer and the buffet.

Gallagher's was packed again. The three mingled with trainees from Damon and the other firms. The other firm's programs today were similar to Damon's. The general consensus was that it was a waste of time.

The three returned to the bar for another beer. One of the bartenders was the owner.

"Where did you guys get that funny accent?" the owner inquired.

"We're from Texas," John replied.

"Is it true that you carry guns and ride horses to work?"

"Most Texans own guns but it's illegal to carry them unless it's a shotgun or rifle. The only people who ride horses to work are real cowboys, not drugstore cowboys."

"What's a real cowboy?"

"It's a person who lives on a ranch and works cattle with his horse. He also repairs fences, harvests hay, and does numerous other chores."

"Have you ever been a cowboy?"

"No, there's no money in it."

"What do they make?"

"Usually, they get room and board, live in a bunk house, and are paid minimum wage."

"That doesn't sound like a movie cowboy."

"No, it doesn't."

"Why do they do it?"

"Because some of them love the work and isolation and others have no other skills. We're getting hungry. We'll give you some buffet business."

"It's on me."

They thanked him and proceeded to the buffet. After a hearty Irish meal, they returned to the hotel.

The next morning, they resumed the routine of riding the subway to the World Trade Center.

The morning was spent touting the firm's high commission products. The trainees were led to believe that these products were a short road to instant wealth.

The afternoon involved a psychologist informing the group of different personality types and how to close them. He identified four types. They were drivers, expressives, analyticals, and amiables. Drivers were only interested in the bottom line. They had unique characteristics. They seldom smiled. Your conversation with them would be short. If they wore a monogrammed shirt, the monogram would be on the pocket. You closed them by informing them of the projected return of the investment and asking them if they were interested. If they were not, you were wasting your time trying to sell them. These types were loners and would almost never give you referrals. However, they were good prospects because they had money as a result of their drive for success.

The expressives were a different person. They liked people and liked to drop names. If they went to a party, they would know all of the attendees by the end of it. In addition, they would probably become a friend with half of them. If they wore a monogrammed shirt, the monogram would be on the sleeve. You closed him by complimenting him and showing him the potential of the investment. Because of his social skills, he would send you many referrals. This was the ideal client. Make it a point to take him to lunch occasionally and establish a social relationship with him. This would pay dividends.

The analyliticals were difficult. They wanted to analyze everything to death. They wanted written facts and figures on everything. They took a long time to reach a conclusion. Then, they may go over the material again to confirm their conclusions. This type was not a good prospect.

Perhaps the most difficult was the amiable. He wanted to be your friend and was extremely hesitant about making a decision. You can spend a long time with him and never get an order.

The psychologist concludes by saying that drivers and expressives were your best prospects because they can make quick decisions.

On the way back to the hotel, John asked Bob and Joe what they thought of this session.

"It was interesting. I learned some things I didn't know." Bob said

"It was great. Now I can get inside their minds, manipulate them, and generate even more commissions." Joe stated.

"I don't think you're that good as a psychologist yet."

"We'll see."

As they were walking to the hotel, John said that they needed to start experiencing the ethninticity of the city. He suggested they go to China Town for dinner. They agreed to meet at six o'clock.

As they entered restaurant row of China Town, Joe and Bob were amazed by the number of restaurants and the variety of oriental food. After much deliberation, they chose a restaurant. There were items on the menu that they had never seen. Bob asked how to determine what was in the dish. Joe told him to ask the waitress. John recommended that they order something they have not eaten before. After much debate, they finally ordered. The food was good. They finished and returned to the hotel.

On Wednesday, instructions on how to close the sale continued. This session concentrated on overcoming objections to the investment. A consultant spent the morning covering this. He said that when an objection arises; acknowledge it by telling them you understand their concern. Then, tell them why they are wrong. If the objection persists, wear them down by continually giving them more reasons they are wrong. When they appear to weaken, ask for the order. He also pointed out that people were profit centers for you because they generated commissions. He then reflected Mike's philosophy by saying that if you did not get their money, another broker would. He spent the remainder of the morning using overheads to explain different objections and closing scenarios. He concluded by saying that this was the easiest sales job in the world because people actually think you are an expert. He stated that you can go to a party with a car salesman and an insurance salesman in attendance and they will ignore those two and ask you what the market is going to do. What he did not say was that brokers and money managers cannot predict what the market will do. If they could, there would not be any brokers, because they would all be retired as multi-millionaires.

In the afternoon, the trainees paired up and role-played about how to overcome objections.

John, Bob, and Joe were walking through the lobby on their way to the subway.

"What did you guys think about that program?" Bob asked.

"It was excellent. I'm learning more and more about how to get into their minds and manipulate them." Joe replied

"I don't believe in manipulation," John said. "If you find out what their financial goals are and satisfy those goals, they'll be long term clients."

"You'll starve to death."

"I don't think so."

"I agree with John," Bob said. "You must satisfy the needs of your clients."

"My needs come first," Joe replied. "I want a lot of money in my pocket."

"Joe, I predict that you'll lose your license within the year," John said.

"No chance."

Thursday, a telemarketing consultant was present. The morning was spent listening to her philosophy of telemarketing. Since brokers get most of their clients over the phone, this was an important subject. She stated that the more calls you make, the more successful you will be. She suggested a minimum of one hundred calls a day for new brokers. She said that ninety percent of all calls were answered before the fourth ring. Therefore, to save time, hang up after the third ring. She then related that, during a phone call, you had ten seconds to get their attention. If it took longer than that, you would not be able to strike up a conversation. She suggested that, after introducing yourself, say something exciting, such as, "I want to tell you about a great investment. Are you interested in making money?" She says that if they were not interested in money, they were brain dead. She strongly recommended qualifying the prospect to determine if they were liquid. Ask them, "If you see an investment you really like, can you invest twenty thousand now?" She said to compile a list of two hundred qualified prospects and call them regularly. If they become clients or you gave up on them, add new ones to keep the list at two hundred.

The trainees were required to bring a call list to the training session. In the afternoon, phones were hooked up and everybody made calls while the consultant critiqued them.

They all started towards the subway.

"What did you two think about that session?" Joe asked.

"I think it was productive," Bob replied. "At least, it didn't concentrate on screwing the public."

"Yeah, I learned some things about managing your prospect list," John said.

"I didn't get a damn thing out of it," Joe said. "There's no way I'm going to maintain a two hundred name calling list. I'll tell them what they want to hear during the first call or two and close them."

"Is what they want to hear always the truth?"

"John, that's irrelevant. My job is to generate commissions. Ask Mike."

"You're a nice person."

"My mother thinks so."

"She's generous."

They go to Gallagher's. John strikes up a conversation with Mary, a trainee from another firm.

"How's it going?" John asked.

"Not well. They don't seem to care about the client."

"You're apparently getting some of the same propaganda we are."

"I'm considering getting out of this business."

"Don't do that. Give it a chance. You don't have to follow the screw the client line."

"That makes sense."

"We could always become used car sales persons."

Mary laughed.

"What do they make?"

"That depends on your ability to lie."

"What's different?"

"The heat on the car lot during the summer."

"You're crazy."

"That's better than being insane."

"Let's get together for a beer sometime."

"OK."

Friday was dedicated to the fine art of moving money. This involved switching from one investment to another to generate more commissions. Local veteran brokers conducted the lesson. The first broker covered stocks. He stated that there was always a reason to switch stocks. If a stock goes down, recommend that the client sell it and switch to a stock that is moving. Tell them that this would recoup their losses. If they do not want to sell, scare them out of the stock. Use your computer to call up news on the stock. Find something that was not positive and tell them that it could dramatically affect the price. If the stock goes up, tell them to take their profit and move into a stock with better potential. Again, if they hesitate, use the news ploy. What he did not say is that statistics prove that one's return on stocks is maximized by holding them long term.

The next broker touted stock and index options. An option was a right to buy at a predetermined price and had a time limit. She said that options were the greatest commission generators in the history of the stock market. They were volatile and moved up and down quickly. Therefore, you always had an excuse to trade them. She explained different types of options, but the theme was moving the money. She did not reveal that because options are depreciating assets, eighty percent of investors lose money on them.

The next broker related how to move money invested in bonds. His vehicle was a bond swap. This involved selling a bond and buying a bond of similar value. The investor must have had a loss on the bond he was selling. This enabled him to take a tax write off and essentially maintain his original position. This was the only strategy that is brought up that made sense.

The last broker discussed mutual funds. He states that most investors bought funds for the long haul. He then said that you could change this. You could always find a fund that was performing better than the one they were in. Switch them to one of these. He pointed out that funds were high commission items and that you could make a lot of money doing this. This was the worst advice of the day.

They were on their way back to the hotel.

"What do you guys want to do this weekend?" John asked.

"Let's go to Atlantic City and roll the dice," Joe replied.

"Sounds good to me."

"I've never been to a casino," Bob said.

"Don't worry about it. It's a unique experience. Just don't bet much because you're probably going to lose. People watching is the fun part."

They checked around and discovered that a hotel in the next block had a bus that goes there. The fare was twenty dollars and you received twenty dollars in chips. They made reservations on the bus.

They went to Gallagher's for dinner. John bumped into Mary.

"How did your day go?" Mary asked.

"It could have been better. We covered moving money today." John answered.

"Yeah, we got into a little bit of that crap today."

"How's everything else going with you?"

"OK. I've just realized that I'm extremely attracted to you."

"Thanks for the compliment. You're an attractive woman."

"My roommate is out-of-town this weekend. Let's spend the weekend together."

"I can't."

"Why?"

"I'm very married. Are you?"

"Yes, but who'll know?"

"We will."

"You're too moral. But I'm not giving up."

The next morning, the three Damon trainees boarded the bus and headed for Atlantic City. It was an interesting trip. There was a blind lady with her dog sitting at the front of the bus near the driver. The dog barked. The driver yelled at the dog. This excited the dog and she started barking constantly. The driver became furious. He screamed to the blind lady that if the fucking dog did not shut up, he would stop and put both of them off the bus. The blind lady was in tears. She told the driver that she needs her dog to lead her. The driver replied that he did not give a shit.

John was sitting next to Bob.

"Bob, I've had all I can take," John said.

He proceeded to the driver.

"If you make one more remark to either the lady or the dog, I'll whip your ass unmercifully." John said.

"You're bluffing"

"You can pull the bus over and we'll settle it on the side of the road or I can get a friend to drive it and we'll finish it on the bus. Which do you prefer?"

"I think this has all been a misunderstanding. Are you willing to drop it?"

"Yes, if you agree not to harass the blind lady or her dog."

"That's not a problem."

John returned to his seat.

"Would you have done it?" Bob asked.

"In a heartbeat. Sometime, you must stand up for what's right. There are too many people in our society that don't care." John said.

They arrived in Atlantic City. They disembarked and started towards the casino. On the way, the blind lady thanked John for his help. John told her that it was his pleasure and wished her good luck on the tables.

Everyone had a good time. The only winner in the Damon group was Bob, who won close to a hundred dollars. Joe and John needled him.

"It's beginner's luck," John said.

"Yeah, and your history of clean living probably contributed as well. With God on your side, it's impossible to lose." Joe added.

Bob laughed.

"Let's come back next weekend," Bob said. "This is easy money."

"No way," Joe said. "I'm tapped out. Also, I don't have the influence with higher powers that you do."

They boarded the bus and returned to the hotel. The Damon three were hungry and walked to Gallagher's. The usual crowd was there. Mary approached John and asked him what he did today. John told her. She said that she might go there tomorrow. John informed her of the bargain bus ride. She said thanks and leaves. Bob, Joe, and John ate and returned to the hotel. They were tired as a result of the Atlantic City excursion.

Monday, the training session covered prospecting, or how to put together an effective call list. The consultant said you must be creative so you were not calling the same people who everybody else was. Furthermore, you must call prospects with money. If you do not, you are wasting your time. He suggested getting a list of airplane owners and people who own sailboats. In addition, find prospects with large real estate holdings. Another source was wealthy neighborhoods. He explained what publication you can use to get phone numbers by street. He then related that a lot of these numbers would be unlisted. He told the trainees how to get these unlisted numbers. He also mentioned that country club and gun club membership lists were good sources. Also, watch the business section of the newspaper for higher-level promotions. He concluded by saying to use your imagination to come up with unusual sources.

The remainder of the week and the last two weeks were devoted to reinforcing and adding to what was covered during the first six days.

The morning of the last day, the President of the firm gave a pep talk. Then, everybody left for the airport to go home.

CHAPTER 3

They reported to the office on Monday. Mike congratulated them for finishing their training. He then gave them a handout listing the minimum commission standards for the next six months. Mike's secretary escorted them to their desks. They organized their desks and got on the phones.

They almost never got off the phone during the first month. They made their commission standards. Joe led the pack in commissions.

Mike called them into his office and complimented them on meeting their standards. He then told them that they should mingle with the veteran brokers and learn their tactics. He said to start with the big producers such as Sue Thomason and Jim Rabin.

The next day, John decided to get with Sue. She was a piece of work. She wore an identical blue suit to work each day. She was also so unattractive that none of the men gave her a second look. However, she generated large commissions. John wanted to find out how she did it.

John approached Sue and asked if he could observe and asked some questions. She said yes and directed him to sit down. She stated that most of her business involved mutual funds. She then told John something he already knew. The firm's funds were no load and the outside funds were front-end loads. That meant that a no load fund had no commissions but had higher management fees and there was a penalty for selling within five years. The load funds required a commission up front but there is no penalty for selling. In addition, the management fees were much less.

Sue picked up the phone. While dialing, she told John that this client was in a load fund.

"Listen to me. You'll learn something," Sue said.

She dials the phone.

"Tom, this is Sue. How are you today?"

"I'm great. What's on your mind?"

"We have a minor problem, but there's a solution."

"What's the problem?"

"When I put your fifty thousand into the fund, I didn't know that the fund manager would resign the next week. He's one of the best. I'm very concerned about the future performance of this fund. I recommend that you switch to another fund."

"I don't want to pay another six percent commission."

"You'll not need to. Even though I had no way of knowing about this change, I feel badly about it because you're a valued client. Therefore, I've been granted permission to put you in a similar Damon fund commission free. Is that fair?"

"Yeah, that dog will hunt."

"OK, I'll do it now."

"Thanks for your help."

"That's my job."

Sue hung up the phone and raised her arms like a referee giving a touchdown signal in the end zone.

"That was great. I've generated six thousand in commissions from this guy in two weeks. That's eighteen hundred in my pocket," Sue stated.

"You switched him within two weeks?" John asked.

"Yeah, is that great or what?"

"Did the fund manager really quit?"

"What difference does it make? The key to this game is to put them in a load fund to start with. You then switch them to a no load fund and make them feel like you're doing them a favor. Listen to this call."

She went through her client records and found one with seventy five thousand dollars in a government securities fund. She dialed the phone.

"Hi Becky. This is Sue."

"How are you today Sue?"

"I'm great, and you?"

"It's going well. My new medication has made my arthritis much better."

"That's wonderful. How are the grandchildren?"

"They're a joy. I can't wait for each visit."

"I'm looking forward to having grandchildren of my own."

"You'll enjoy them."

"Becky, I called because there is a problem with your fund. It's been alleged that there are mismanagement problems. This has come to light after I recommended the fund."

"I'm scared. You know that's the only money I have and that I depend on the interest for my retirement."

"Yes, and I sincerely care about you. Therefore, I've made arrangements to put you in a fund with a slightly higher yield and commission free. Is that fair?"

"I don't know. I need to talk to my son."

"Becky, the information I'm getting is that the fund will face serious difficulties any day now. We must do something now."

"Let me think about it."

"That could use valuable time and result in a loss on your investment. Do want that?"

"No."

"Becky, I care about you. I don't want to be responsible for the loss of your retirement income. My manager is whimsical. He may change his mind on the free commission at any moment. Why don't we protect your retirement and do this today?"

"OK."

"I'll take care of it for you. Give your grandchildren a kiss from me."

"I will. Thanks for your help."

"That's my job. I'll talk to you later."

Sue raises her fist in the air as a token of celebration.

"That was a tough close. I'm on a roll. Let's see if I can get even more commissions."

She again thumbed through her client records.

"This guy needs a change."

She dialed the phone.

"Bill, this is Sue. What the hell is going on with you?"

"I'm in alligators up to my ass. This business is about to kill me."

"I know you well enough to know that you're making money."

"Yeah, but it's killing me. What's on your mind?"

"We need to change funds. There are problems with the fund you're in."

"What kind of problems?"

"The fund manager may be indicted for misappropriating money."

"I think that's bullshit. I'll do my own research."

"Bill, you're taking a chance on losing money on your investment."

"I bought this fund for the long haul. If this guy steals the money, I'll sue your ass and Damon for not checking the fund out."

"I can get you into another fund without a commission."

"What's the management fee?"

"One and half percent."

"What's the fee on the fund I'm in?"

Sue hesitates.

"I'm not sure, but I think it's about a half percent."

"You're trying to churn me. I'm transferring my account."

"Don't do that. Let's have lunch tomorrow."

"Forget it."

Bill hung up.

Churning was known in the trade as moving money for the sole purpose of generating commissions.

Sue laughed.

"I just lost a one hundred thousand dollar account. You win some, lose some, and some are rained out. He's too knowledgeable. That's not the type of client I want." Sue said.

"Do you think it's right to switch investments for the purpose of generating commissions?" John asked.

"I have a house, a car, and a disabled Father to support. How else can I maintain my lifestyle and meet my commitments?"

"You could become an honest broker."

"You're an asshole. You'll never make it in this business. Get the hell out of here."

John left.

In the meantime, Sue called Mike. Mike asked John to come to his office.

"I understand that you insulted Sue." Mike stated.

"In what way?" John asked.

"She says that you accused her of being dishonest."

"That's an accurate statement."

"Why did you do that?"

"Do you know what she's doing?"

"Yeah, but she's one of my biggest producers. As long as I don't get a lot of complaints, I'll not worry about it."

"Have you gotten any complaints?"

"That's confidential."

"I suppose that I'm learning some of the unwritten rules."

Mike chuckled.

"John, don't insult other brokers. There's even honor among thieves."

Mike laughed heartily.

"I don't think that's funny."

"You'll get over it. Get out there and generate some commissions."

John left and resumed making phone calls.

The next day, he decided to visit with Jim. He was a stock jockey. That means he trades stocks.

John approached him and asked if he would tutor him.

"Sure, sit down," Jim said.

"What's your philosophy?" John asked.

"You sell them a stock, hold it for a short period of time, and sell it.

In conjunction with the sale, you switch them into another stock. This doubles your commissions."

"Are your clients making money with this strategy?"

"Some of them are. But that's not the point. I'm making a lot of money. Once they start trading, they're like fish. They get the hook in their mouth and don't give up. It's an addiction."

"Show me your talent."

Jim smiled. He picks up the phone and calls a client with a two-dollar gain on a twenty-dollar stock.

"Tom, this is Jim. What's happening in your world?"

"Nothing but the lease. What's up?"

"Unfortunately, I have bad news on one of your stocks."

"Which one?"

"Diablo."

"What's the news?"

"It just came across the wire that they lost a big account. I called you immediately. That gives us a chance to take profits before selling starts. I suggest that we invest the proceeds in STL Corporation. It was put on our recommended list today. That almost guarantees a rise in price because every broker in the firm will be pushing it. We need to do something immediately."

"Do it."

"I'll call you back and confirm the trades. I'll talk to you within ten or fifteen minutes. Bye."

"Is that what you call moving money?" John asked.

"Yeah, isn't it great?"

"Great for whom?"

"Great for me."

"What about the client?"

"He made money on the trade."

"Would he have made more money if he had held the stock longer?"

"Who knows? I'm no fortune teller."

"Statistically, the longer you hold the stock, the greater your return."

"That's bullshit. The financial columnists print that crap to discredit brokers. I think they all have a latent desire to be brokers."

Jim thumbed through his client records (known in the business as a book). He smiled and told John that his system would also work in a loss situation. He dials the phone.

"Arthur, Jim here. What's happening?"

"Not a hell of a lot that's good. How about you?"

"Things are going well. Arthur, as you know, I try to keep you informed on your investments. We have a loss on Inco. I recommend that we sell it and buy Atcel. There's a lot of good things happening with this stock and I'm confident that we'll more than recoup our losses."

"What's this we stuff? It's my money. I think I'll weather it out and see what happens."

"I use we because I consider you a friend and a valued client. I also use it because I feel responsible for giving you the best advice possible. As a result, I feel that we're in this together. I wouldn't give you advice that I wouldn't give to my mother. Does that make sense?"

"Yeah, I guess so."

"Hold on Arthur. There's news about Inco coming over the wire."

"What is it?"

"They're facing major lawsuit's. I suspected that. We need to make the trade and cut our losses while we can."

"OK, but this better work or I'm history."

"Trust me. I'll call you with the confirmation."

Jim hung up.

"How did you like that work of art?" Jim asked.

"I didn't see news about lawsuits," John replied.

"What difference does it make? He'll never know the difference. Meanwhile, I made a big commission."

"Is that right?"

"What's right is survival in this business and paying your bills. You'll learn that."

"Maybe, but I hope not. Thanks for your time."

"No problem."

John returned to his desk in disgust.

Bob and Joe have also observed the two brokers. Bob, like John, is disgusted. Joe is enthusiastic because he believes that he has learned some new tricks that will increase his commissions.

CHAPTER 4

J ohn decided to concentrate on retirement accounts. These involved large sums of money. Also, they lent themselves to conservative long-term investments, which suited John's preference. He did not want to churn. He compiled a list of the Human Resource managers of local corporations. He contacted them and revealed his credentials. He then offered to conduct free seminars for groups or to meet with the retiring employees personally. Overall, the response was good.

His first seminar was at a major corporation and he had five people present. They all had a 401K. He explained that if they took the money out of the 401K, they would be required to pay taxes on the entire amount. He stated that was an onerous tax burden, but there was an alternative. They could roll the funds into an IRA. Then, they paid taxes only on what they withdrew, but there was a ten percent penalty. If they were fifty-nine or older, they cold take the money out without a penalty. In the meantime, the funds in the IRA earned money tax-free.

He then explained his investment philosophy. He said that his main goal was to protect their retirement. Therefore, his focus would be on conservative investments with decent earnings. They would be held for the long term. He asked if there were any questions at this point.

"What do you mean by a conservative investment?" someone asked.

"I mean an investment with low risk. This will protect your capital, which you are depending on for your retirement," John replied.

"Give me some examples."

"First of all, we will not do any stock or option trading. If you're into that, find another broker. We will deal exclusively with mutual funds. This enables you to receive professional money management. Examples are Ginnie Mae funds, which are guaranteed by the government, and utility funds, which are not that volatile and have very high yields."

"How do we know that we can trust you?" another attendee asked.

"I spent twenty-five years in the business world. I received a 401K settlement just as you'll do in the near future. Mine is invested the way we talked about. I feel secure about my retirement."

"If you put your money where your mouth is, that's good enough for me."

"Are there any more questions?"

"How do we get an appointment with you?"

"I'm going to mingle with you now and we can make appointments then."

John mingled with the group and made three appointments. He then returned to the office.

As he went to his desk, Mike told him to come to his office.

"You were gone from the office a long time. How did it go?" Mike asked.

"I think it went well. There were five people there and I have appointments with three of them." John replied

"These are retirement accounts, right?"

"Yes."

"What do you intend to put them in?"

"Conservative, long term investments. All the investments will be mutual funds."

"How will you move the money?"

"I don't intend to. This money is their life savings and their retirement security."

"You're missing the boat."

"In what way?"

"The purpose of this business is to generate commissions. You can't do that by letting the money sit there."

"I refuse to lie and cheat for commissions. If you think I should, fire me now."

"That's not the intention of this meeting. I'm curious about your strategy."

"My strategy is to protect their retirement. By doing this, I'll get referrals and have a steady stream of commissions."

"That's idealistic, but who knows, it may work. Good luck with it."

"Thanks."

John returned to his desk. He had a message from Leslie, who attended the seminar. John called her.

"Leslie, this is John. What can I do for you?" John asked.

"I'm getting my money today. What should I do?" Leslie asked.

"Don't take a check. To prevent taxes, you must transfer the funds from one trustee to another. You already have an appointment tomorrow. I'll have all the paperwork ready and show you how to fill it out."

"I'm nervous. Can I come in earlier?"

"Sure, what time?"

"As early as possible."

"Let me look. OK, I come in at eight and don't have anything then. Is that OK with you?"

"Perfect. I'll see you then."

"Don't be nervous. I'll walk you through everything."

"I appreciate that. I'll see you tomorrow morning."

"I'm looking forward to it."

John hung up.

The next morning, Leslie came in. She had five hundred thousand dollars to invest. John put her in various conservative investments and informed her that it would take about a week for the money to be transferred. She thanked him and left.

Later in the day, he met with Brian. Brian had six months before he retires. He was seeking information. John explained all of his options, including investment options. Brian was impressed and says that they would do business when he retired.

Then, John visited with Paul. He was also receiving his settlement and had three hundred thousand dollars to invest. They had a lengthy conversation and Paul agreed to invest. They filled out the paper work for the transfer. His money would also arrive next week.

John spent the remainder of the week contacting more Human Resource managers.

The following week, two days before the end of the month, the transfers arrived. John dropped (executed) the tickets (trade slips). He generated forty thousand in commissions. With his other commissions, he led the office that month.

Suddenly, he was Mike's golden boy. Mike called him to his office. He shook John's hand and patted him on the back.

"I told you that you would be a good broker. I wouldn't have dreamed that you would have this kind of production this soon. You're a special talent," Mike said.

"I appreciate the compliment," John replied

"What exactly are you doing?"

"The right thing."

Mike laughed.

"How are you getting your leads for these big accounts?"

"Through my network."

"You must have a hell of a network."

"I do."

"Let's take our wives out to dinner on Friday. It's on me."

"I'd like that, but my wife works late on Fridays and she is in no mood to go out. We're going out-of-town this weekend. Maybe we can do it next week."

"That sounds good. Get out there and drop some more big tickets."

John left. He hoped that Mike would forget the dinner invitation because he did not want to spend an evening with him. John intentionally lied about his lead sources because he knew that Mike would tell the other brokers. As a result, he would have competition. He thought that the other brokers should be creative and come up with their own sources.

John was also a hot commodity with the other brokers. Joe came to his desk.

"You're a super star," Joe said. "What are you doing?"

"I'm putting them in conservative investments for the long term," John answered.

"That's bullshit and you know it. You can't generate those kinds of commissions doing that."

"Trust me. I did."

"Come on. We went through training together and we're friends. Tell me what's going on."

"I already have."

"Then tell me where you're getting all this money."

"If I told you that, you'd be after the same sources."

"No I wouldn't. I'm just curious."

"Yeah, right."

"Let's have lunch tomorrow. I'll spring for the tab."

"I can't. I'm lunching with a client."

"Then let's have a beer after work. It's on me."

"That's out because I'm taking my wife to dinner tonight."

"You're giving me the run around."

"No I'm not. We'll get together next week."

Joe patted him on the back and congratulated him on his performance. He then left.

Most of the other brokers sought out John and asked about his sources. He did not reveal them to anyone. He got numerous lunch and bar invitations. He thought to himself that he could eat and drink free for a month. He did not think that taking the largess without revealing information was right.

Bob decided to specialize in tax-free municipal bonds and mutual funds. He was calling high-income individuals and was getting some bond business. He called middle class people to solicit mutual fund sales. He was doing reasonably well but was struggling to meet his quota. His trademark was honesty.

The following month, Bob was far below his quota. Mike called him to his office.

"What's the problem?" Mike asked.

"I had a bad month. It happens to the best of us," Bob answered.

"It can't happen much in this business. What do you intend to do to improve your performance?"

"I'm not sure. I probably need to improve my closing skills."

"I don't think that's the solution. I've noticed that almost all your business is municipal bonds and mutual funds. It's difficult to move that money. I suggest that you trade stocks and options. You can move that money easily. Can you do that?"

"I don't know. I understand that you maximize return on stocks by holding them long term. And since options are a depreciating asset, 80% of investors lose money on them."

"So what, Bob. That's what makes options great. You always have an excuse to switch them. That means commissions. As for stocks, if you time the market right, you maximize the client return."

"Name one person that can time the market. If they could, they would own the country."

"That's beside the point. Have confidence and make them believe that you can time it. Most of them are dummies about the market. Act like the expert."

"Is that honest?"

"Honesty is not the point. Commissions are the point. If you don't earn them, you don't stay in this business. I have confidence in you. I want you to try what we talked about. OK?"

Bob hesitated. He realizes that if he does not agree, he will probably be fired.

"Yes, I can do that."

"Good. You're a good man. Get out there out and do it to them. You'll be surprised at the results."

Bob left wondering if he wanted to stay in this business.

Joe was exceeding his quota. He did anything to generate commissions. He traded stocks and options. He sold mutual funds and limited partnerships. He would also sell bonds if that were all the client would buy. He started by calling a prospect and introducing himself as a long time broker who made money for his clients. He told them he was not trying to sell them anything today but that he had been watching a promising investment and doing research to determine if it would yield a substantial return for his clients. He then asked them if they really liked the investment, did they have at least ten to twenty thousand dollars to invest now. If yes, he told them that he would call them if his research indicates a substantial return.

Joe picked up the phone and dialed.

"Ed, this is Joe at Damon," Joe said.

"What's going on?" Ed asked

"A lot. I told you that if I found an excellent investment, I'd call you. I've found it."

"What is it?"

"It's a little known stock in the high tech industry. They're profits are soaring. We need to get in now before the institutional investors catch wind of it and drive the price up. I've already put part of my Mother's retirement funds in the stock."

"What's the name of it?"

"Axal. It's on the NASDAQ, so you can follow it."

"Give me a hundred shares."

"Ed, it's only selling for ten dollars a share. You can get two thousand shares for twenty thousand. It'll be a big winner. Do you think I would risk my Mother's retirement?"

"Give me a thousand shares. That's as far as I'm going."

"You made a wise decision. I'll call you with the confirmation."

"Wait a minute. How long have you been a broker?"

"A long time. Let me think. About fifteen years."

"Then you should know what you're doing. Go ahead and do it."

"I appreciate the business. I'll treat you right. If you'll stick with me, we'll make a lot of money. There may be some ups and downs, but we'll make money."

"You better be right."

"I am. I'll call you when the trade is confirmed."

Joe hung up. This call was typical of Joe's calls.

The next day, Bob asked John to have lunch with him. John agreed and asked him what was on his mind. Bob told him that they would talk about it.

They went to a local restaurant and ordered. Bob told John about his conversation with Mike.

"That sounds like him. He doesn't seem to care about employees or clients," John said.

"I've thought about this overnight. I think I'll quit today," Bob said.

"Don't do that. This business needs honest people like you."

"Yeah, but I can't stomach the deception and the lying that is apparently necessary to be successful."

"Just ignore it. Raise a lot funds for legitimate investments and the commissions will follow."

"That's easy for you to say because you're doing it. My sales talents aren't that good."

"Bob, what can I do to change your mind?"

"Nothing."

"What will you do?"

"I'm going back to the ministry. At the least, I'll be helping people and not screwing them."

"Bob, I hate this. You're a friend and I've always admired your principles. There's not any people in Damon that I want to be friends with."

"You'll eventually find a few."

They paid their tabs and left. When they got back to the office, Bob walked into Mike's office and resigned.

"What the hell's this," Mike shouted. "I thought we had a deal."

"My conscience will not let me carry out the deal," Bob replied.

"So you're not man of your word?"

"To the contrary, I refuse to deceive and lie to get a sale."

"Do you think that telling the client that you think this a good investment is deceitful?"

"Yes, if you don't believe it."

"I've invested all this money in you and you're going to bail out?"

"Yes."

"That's not right."

"Yes it is. You probably would have fired me in the next two months for lack of production. I'm not suited for this business."

"You may be right. I wish you good luck."

"Thanks."

Bob left, gathered his belongings, and exited the building.

The original four were now down to two.

Joe receives his first complaint from a client. Mike called him to his office.

"Do you know about the complaint from Brenda Jacobson?" Mike asked.

"Yes," Joe answered.

"What transpired?"

"I told her that I thought the stock was a good investment."

"What else did you say?"

"I told her that I believed that the stock would go up by 20% within two weeks."

"How did you know that?"

"I just felt it."

"Joe you erred. You can't tell a client something like that."

"Then how in the hell am I going to make a sale?"

"Use different terminology. Say I believe that you will receive a substantial return on your investment within a short period. That's subjective and they can't nail you on it. What's the definition of substantial? What's the definition of a short period? Do you get the gist of this?"

"Yes, it makes sense."

"Damon will be required to pay for her losses and a complaint will be entered on your license history."

"I'm sorry I messed up, Mike."

Mike patted him on the back.

"Don't worry about it. I'll take care of it. Keep those commissions flowing."

"I will. Thanks for your help Mike."

"No problem."

Joe returned to his desk.

CHAPTER 5

Damon decided to push limited partnerships. In these, the investor has no liability, except his investment. The general partner assumed the bill on other liabilities if the partnership got in trouble. These partnerships covered several areas, including commercial real estate, oil and gas drilling, and more exotic investments.

Gary Robinson, the firm's guru on partnerships, flew to Dallas from New York to sell his wares. All the branch brokers went to the meeting room to hear his pitch.

Gary introduced himself and said that he had good news. All of the partnerships would pay a minimum of eight percent commission. He first touted the real estate deals. Almost all of them consisted of office buildings. He cited expected returns of up to forty percent. He then stated that everybody wanted to own real estate; so this was an easy sale with high commissions. He said that if you told them the projected return and that they will own a piece of America, it was a done deal. Also, eight percent commission is generated. He asked if there were any questions at this point.

"How did you arrive at a forty percent return?" one of the brokers asked.

"When I give you the handouts at the end of the meeting, you'll understand. The strategy is to build a first class high rise, lease it fully, and then sell it at a huge profit." Gary answered.

"What if they can't lease all of the space?"

"That's not a possibility. As hot as the real estate market is, it's a given that they'll lease it."

"But what if they don't?"

"Don't worry about it. Sell it and make money for yourself and your client."

Gary then touted oil and gas drilling. He said that these were ideal for high-income investors because of tax benefits such as depletion. He related that these investments would provide an income for several years as the oil and gas is pumped from the ground. He then stated that Texans all wanted to own part of an oil well. This should be a very easy sell. Push the tax benefits and the long-term income stream. He asked if there were any questions.

"Dry holes are drilled every day," said a broker. "How will you cope with that?"

"We'll probably get a couple. However, we'll have the funds to weather it. The main thing is that we'll be drilling in known oil fields and will have some of the best geologists in the world." Gary replied.

"Where did you find these guys? In the middle east?" All the oil production has gone overseas."

"They're not on board yet, but they will be. We'll pay them whatever it takes. There's a tremendous amount of oil left in the US. When we find it, we'll have a gold mine."

"This sounds risky to me."

"Life is a risk. You can't hit a home run without taking a big swing. The potential profits are gigantic. Do your clients a favor and put them in these oil and gas deals. You'll also be doing yourself a favor by earning large commissions. Isn't that the name of the game?"

Gary then began to unveil his crown jewel. He said that the brokers would love this one because it paid a ten percent commission. Also, it was the closest thing to a sure thing that they would ever see. The project involved deploying hundreds of windmills in northern California. They were used to generate electricity. He related that they could produce electricity for a third of the cost of conventional methods. He then revealed that a large utility had contracted to buy all of the production at slightly below conventional cost. He then told them to run the numbers and they would determine that there are huge profits to be had.

"What do they do when the wind is not blowing?" a broker asked.

"No problem. They'll be located on hills where the wind blows constantly." Gary answered.

"Good. I live on a hill. My electricity bills are high. Where do I get one of these devices?"

All the brokers laughed. Gary chuckled.

"Seriously, the area where they will be deployed is known for constant wind. Why else would the utility company make a commitment?"

"Has this been tried before?" another broker asked.

"Good question. It has been used successfully in Europe. In fact, that's where they're buying the windmills. This is something new in this country that will be a huge success."

"How long do these things last," a broker asked.

"Another excellent question. In Europe, with routine maintenance they last for years."

"Do mean they never break down?"

"No. Like any machine, they occasionally break down. However, this is factored into the cost of production. This investment is a sure winner."

Gary concluded by saying that these investments are designed to make money for both the client and the broker.

As the brokers left, about half of them wanted to shun these investments and the other half wanted to sell them because of the high commissions.

John, because of his clientele and his conservative approach, decided to forego the investments. Joe was fired up. He loved the large commissions.

Joe returned to his desk and reviewed the literature for sales tips. He picked up the phone.

"Greg, this is Joe. We're introducing a new investment this week. This is one of the best I've seen in all of my years in the business. Do you want to learn about it?"

"Sure. What is it?"

"It's a limited partnership."

"What's that?"

"That means that you have no liability. If something goes wrong, the general partner picks up the tab. But rest assured that nothing would go wrong on this deal. It's as close to a sure thing as you can get."

"What are they investing in?"

"They'll construct high tech windmills in northern California, where the wind constantly blows, to generate electricity. This has been wildly successful in Europe. Now, here is the clincher. They already have a contract with a large utility to buy all of their production at about three times their production costs. Is that a winner or not?"

"It sounds good but it's somewhat unusual."

"When Edison invented the light bulb, it was unusual. I'm in and I'm putting my parents in. Greg, this is probably the best investment you'll ever make."

"What's the minimum investment?"

"Five thousand, but this is so good that I recommend at least twenty thousand."

"Put me down for five."

"Greg, you're leaving money on the table."

"I said five."

"Ok, thanks for the business. You'll not regret it. I'll talk to you later."

Joe dials again. He thinks he is on a roll.

"Hi Bill. How are you?"

"I'm doing great. And you?"

"Things are going very well because we have a tremendous new investment."

"What is it?"

Joe explained the windmill project to him.

"That's the largest pile of bullshit I've ever smelled. There are more holes in that deal than there are in Swiss cheese."

"What do you mean? This is an excellent investment."

"Don't call me again."

Bill hung up.

Joe mumbled to himself that Bill was an idiot. Then he made two more calls concerning the windmills and they both flopped. He decided to go to lunch, have a couple of drinks, forget the windmills, and concentrate on real estate.

He returned from lunch and began making calls on the real estate deals. He dialed the phone.

"Betty, this is Joe. How's my favorite client doing?"

"Flattery will get you everywhere."

They both laughed.

"I have a tremendous new investment to offer you."

"Tell me about it."

He explained the details of a real estate partnership.

"I don't know," Betty said.

"Betty, this is close to a sure thing. I'm personally investing heavily in it."

"I'm too old to make long term investments."

"This is not long term. They'll build the complexes, lease them fully, and then sell at a tremendous profit."

"I'll pass on this one."

"Betty, you're making a mistake."

"Maybe I am, but I'm not going to do it."

"OK. I'll call when a more suitable investment comes. Thanks for your time."

"You're welcome. I'll talk to you later."

Joe made fifteen more calls and sold one unit of a real estate deal. For his work this day, he put three hundred dollars in his pocket.

The office sold a large amount of the partnerships. Mike was jubilant. However, within six months, the windmill project was bankrupt because of equipment failures. Two of the real estate deals and the oil and gas project were in trouble.

Gary returned to Dallas in an attempt to put out the fires. He started by saying that he had not been to AA in ten years but had to go last night. He said that this was the worst experience of his life. He blamed everything on poor management by the general partners. He stated that they should be hung.

"Why didn't you do due diligence and check out their competency?" a broker asked. "This could have saved our clients money."

"We did. Their credentials were impeccable." Gary replied.

"Yeah, we observed how well they performed."

The group gets a good laugh out of this one.

"Why don't we refund the money?" another broker asked.

"You know we can't do that. Those people knew they were taking a risk."

"You told us that the windmill deal was as close to a sure thing as we would ever see. A large number of us conveyed that information to our clients."

"I'm sorry. I was wrong. I believed it at the time."

"You've caused many of us to lose clients," a broker said. "If you hadn't sold us a bill of goods, we would still have them."

"I'm not feeling well. I need to go to the hotel."

Gary walked out.

Mike got up and berated the brokers for giving Gary a hard time. He said that Gary was only trying to do his job. He also pointed out that they made good commissions and that was the name of the game. What difference did it make if a few clients lost money? I think that they are big boys by now. You and the firm made money, and that was what counts. Now, get out there and get on the phone to generate some commissions.

CHAPTER 6

Early Friday morning, Mike called a meeting and announced that, because of a record month, there was an office party tonight after work. The firm would pay for the party. He said that he had reserved a banquet room at the Four Seasons, a luxury hotel. He then stated there would be plenty to drink and the finger food would also be plentiful. He related that if anybody got too drunk to drive home, the firm would pick up the taxi tab. He told them not to drink themselves into a coma.

The last statement got a chuckle.

Mike told the brokers to get out there and earn some commissions and have a good time tonight.

As they were leaving, one of the brokers stated that he couldn't believe that a party was given to celebrate screwing the clients on the partnership deals.

Another broker replied that life worked that way. He said that we did not know that we had been sold a bill of goods. All he knew was that he had made a large amount of money. He could use it. He then said that he did have sympathy for his clients. He hesitated for a moment. Then he told the other broker that if we worried about our clients making money, we would never make any ourselves.

The other broker told him that his attitude sucked.

They went their separate ways.

Everybody worked hard in anticipation of the party. Apparently, Mike's motivational ploy had reaped benefits.

At this branch, two brokers shared a sales assistant, known as a secretary in other businesses. John's assistant was Terri Crowl. She was not only efficient, but also attractive. She came to John's desk.

"John, will you be my escort tonight? I need someone to keep me out of trouble." Terri said.

John laughs and says, "I don't run an escort service, but I'll keep you out of trouble if you'll do what I say. Is that acceptable?"

"Anything you say is acceptable."

"That's out of character for you. What's the problem?"

"I don't want to be the lone stranger there. I need somebody I trust to hang out with me."

"Don't worry about it. I'll take care of it."

"You're wonderful. I'll see you at the party."

After work, everybody proceeded to the party.

They had a couple of drinks. Then Mike interrupted the party to give a brief speech. He had obviously had more than a couple of drinks.

"I want you to know that you are the best brokers in the industry. I love all of you. You've made me a lot of money and this party is a token of my appreciation. There will be more rewards to come. Each time we have a record month, we'll have a party. The next one will be a cookout at South Fork Ranch. I'll have it catered Texas style. We'll have barbecued brisket and plenty to drink. The only damn things you'll need to do is eat and drink. Go back to partying and have a good time." Mike said.

The party continued. Almost everyone was drinking liberally and partaking of the food. Also, budding romances were emerging.

Joe approached Cynthia Taylor, a female broker.

"How's business?" he asked.

"It could be better. You're putting up larger numbers than I. What are you doing?" Cynthia replied.

"I'm just working hard."

"Where are you getting your leads?"

"From numerous sources. You must diversify. I'll get into detail with you when we have time. But the main reason I approached you was to let you know that I've had my eye on you since day one. You're a very attractive and sexy woman."

"That's strange because I'm also attracted to you. What took you so long?"

Joe laughed and said, "I was intimidated by your good looks."

Cynthia laughed and said, "I call that a lame excuse."

"I'll make it up to you. Let's leave and have a nice dinner."

"Where are we going?"

"What do you like?"

"Seafood."

"Cajun or traditional?"

"Cajun. That's the only real seafood. I'm from Louisiana."

"I've always heard that Louisiana women have webbed feet as a result of living in the swamp. Is that true?"

"Cynthia laughs and says, "If you're lucky, you'll eventually find out."

They left to go to dinner. After dinner, Joe told Cynthia that he had some really nice wine at his apartment and asked if she would like to share it. She agreed.

When they entered the apartment, it was very warm. Joe played with the thermostat to no avail. He attempted to contact either the manager or maintenance man. They had both gone home.

"What the hell," Joe said. "Let's drink the wine. That'll cool us off."

"Sounds good to me." Cynthia replied.

Joe uncorked the wine. They sat on the couch and drank it. Cynthia had more than her share. She said that she was hot. Then she took off her blouse and bra and said that she was cooler now. Joe was dumfounded and excited.

"If you're that hot, you should take all of your clothes off." Joe said.

She took off the remainder of her clothes.

"What about your clothes?" she asked.

Joe reciprocated. They were passionate on the couch and then went to the bedroom to have sex in a pool of sweat. They agreed to get together again and she went home.

In the meantime, the party was going strong. Everybody was having a good time and the drinks were flowing freely. Mike has had too much to drink and was barely mobile. He decided to give another speech and asked the brokers for their attention. Fortunately, the Regional Manager, who attended, told him to sit down. Mike stumbled to a chair and sat down.

John, as promised, hung out with Terri. Many of the brokers were making passes at her. She rejected all of them.

"There are some good looking single men here," John said. "Why are you shunning all of them?"

"I just got out of a relationship that I thought would last forever." Terri replied.

"How long ago?"

"About six months."

"You should be over it by now."

"Yes, but I'm not. However, I think I've found someone."

"That's great."

"John, it's you. You're the first man I've been attracted to since then. I want to have a relationship with you."

"Terri, you know that I'm happily married."

"I plan to change that."

"I don't think so."

"Let's just have an affair. I'll grow on you."

"I would love to, but my conscience will not allow me to do it."

"I feel rejected. What can I do to convince you?"

John laughed and said, "If you convince my wife, you've convinced me."

Terri also laughed and asked, "What are the odds on that?"

"I would guess slim and none. But you're welcome to try."

She smiles and says, "I think not."

"Terri, you're a beautiful woman. You'll find someone. I'll be your best friend and your advisor. Can we leave it at that?"

"Yes. You're a great guy."

Two of the male brokers got into an argument over an account that one of them claimed the other had stolen from him. They got into a fight. Most of the other brokers were in a panic.

"What are you going to do?" Terri asked John.

"Nothing. I enjoy a good fight. We don't have a winner yet." John replied.

Several of the brokers interceded and broke up the fight.

Mike was passed out on the table.

The Regional Manager stated that it was time to go home.

Early Monday morning, Mike called a meeting. He berated the brokers for drinking too much. Then he said that they had cost the branch a fortune in taxi fares. He related that they should act more responsibly at future parties. One of the leading producers asked if he could make a statement.

"Sure," Mike said.

"Mike, you're a good man. You're denigrating us for drinking too much. But when I left, you were passed out on the table. I believe that you had more to drink than any of us," the broker said.

"Maybe, but I had a room rented at the hotel, so I didn't have to go anywhere. Does that make sense?"

"If you were drunk, don't condemn us for it."

"I see your point. However, there's no excuse for fighting."

"I agree with you on that one."

"What do we do to prevent it?"

"I've already talked to the brokers involved. It will not happen again."

"Good. This was a productive meeting. Let's get out there and make some money."

When Mike returned to his office, he had a message from Kent Smith, the Regional Manager. Mike returned the call. Kent told him to come downtown because they needed to talk.

"What about?" Mike asked.

"About the party." Kent replied.

"I'm leaving now."

"I'll see you in about thirty minutes."

Mike walked into Kent's office.

He initiated the conversation by saying, "I apologize for my brokers behavior at the party. I've met with them and read them the riot act."

"I don't want to talk about your brokers. I want to talk about you." Kent said.

"Are you serious?"

"Yes. Leadership starts at the top. You demonstrated none. In fact, you were disgraceful. You drank so much that you passed out. Is that the kind of example you want to set for your brokers?"

"I apologize. It will not happen again."

"I know that it will not because the next time it does, you're history. Do you understand that?"

"Yes."

"Get back to work."

Mike returned to the office, shut his door, and did not come out until everybody left.

CHAPTER 7

Options are a right to buy a stock, for a limited period of time, at a predetermined price. For example, if a stock is selling for thirty dollars, you may be able to buy, for a hundred dollars, a thirty-day option to purchase a hundred shares for thirty-two dollars. You do not need to purchase the stock. Instead, you can sell the option, which has gone up in value in proportion to the stock. Obviously, you have a large leverage factor, if you guess right. The drawback is that, because of the time limitations, options are a depreciating asset. As a result, approximately 80% of options investors lose money.

One can also write options. This means that you sell options on stock that you do not own. You are betting that the stock will go down. The major problem is that, since you do not own the stock, the risks incurred are almost unlimited. You can also sell an option that bets that the stock will go down and the risks are the same. These options are known in the trade as naked options.

Ed Jordan considered himself the branch guru on options. He would sell anything, probably including his wife, but he was hooked on the fact that he could move money quickly in options. His complaints were mounting to the critical stage but he did not seem to care.

Joe asked Ed if he could listen in and learn some tricks.

"Yeah, I'm always happy to help new brokers." Ed replied.

Ed dialed the phone.

"Lydia, Ed here."

"Hi Ed. How are you?"

"I'm great."

"How are my stocks doing?"

"They're doing well. I have some good news for you."

"What's that?"

"You have an opportunity to fill your pockets full of money in a hurry."

"How?"

"I've been following a stock for a while. My sources tell me that it is about to make a dramatic rise any day. Because of insider trading rules, I can't tell you the details."

"I have two questions. One is how I will make all this money that quickly? The other is how do you know the stock will make a dramatic move in the near future?"

"I'll answer the second question first. My source has given me five tips and all have paid off handsomely. We'll make money in a hurry by buying options."

"What are options?"

"They're a right to buy a stock at a preset price during a predetermined time frame. For example, this stock is currently trading at fifteen dollars. We can buy an option to purchase a thousand shares at a price of seventeen dollars for five hundred dollars. I expect the stock to go to at least to twenty-five dollars. That means that you will pocket eight thousand within thirty days, which is the time frame I'm recommending for the option."

"I don't know. I haven't done this before."

"I promise you that it's painless. We need to do it today because my source says that the stock could start moving in the next day or two. We'll miss the boat if we don't get in now."

"Can I do five hundred shares?"

"Sure. I'll execute the trade and keep you posted."

"OK."

They hung up.

"What did you think of that?" Ed asked Joe.

"A work of art. Tell me your source. I want to get in on the deals. I'll pay him." Joe replied.

"I don't have a source. I needed to make a sale. If you tell them what they want to hear, you make a sale."

"Joe laughs. I've already learned something from you."

"Hang around and you'll learn more. My next call is to a guy who's trading options and losing big time. I'm about to lose him as a client. Therefore, I intend to milk all of the commissions possible out of him. Listen to this one."

Ed dialed the phone.

"Nick, this is Ed. How's everything going?"

"It could be better. I'm tired of losing money on options."

"I have a solution."

"What's that?"

"We've been trading stock options. We need to be trading index options because the overall market is much easier to predict than individual stocks. I have a strategy to ensure that you make money. It's get even time."

"What the hell is an index option?"

"They're just like stock options except they are tied to the various stock indexes, such as the S&P 500. You can choose which index you want to trade."

"What's this strategy that you mentioned?"

"We'll do a straddle."

"How does that work?"

"We'll buy two options at the same strike price (the price one can exercise the option at). One will be long; so we can make money if the market goes up. The other will be short; so we can make money if the market goes down. We'll make money both ways. Since the overall market is so easy to predict, we'll sell each option when the market peaks in either direction. As a result, we'll win both ways. I've used this strategy with tremendous success."

"Why haven't you told me about this before?"

"Because you like to call your own shots on most of your trades and I didn't want to tick you off. You're a good client."

"I'll try anything once. What are the damages?"

"I will not invest more than two thousand on the first trade. This will give you a chance to gain confidence."

"Do it, but this needs to work."

"OK, I'll keep you informed."

The conversation ended.

"How did you like that maneuvering?" Ed asked Joe.

"You're a master. You keep them in the palm of your hand."

Ed chuckled and gave Joe a high five. The phone rang. It was a call from Becky.

"Becky, how are the kids doing?" Ed asked.

"Not too well." Becky said.

"What happened?"

"You've cost me five thousand dollars trading these stupid options. My accountant says that you have put me in a high risk investment without informing me of the risks."

"Becky, I've got your best interests in mind. Let's trade some more and I'll get your money back."

"No way. I've already been burned. I'm filing a complaint."

Becky hung up and called Mike.

Ed told Joe that you always get a few disgruntled clients. Joe responded that she seemed more than disgruntled. Ed said that he needed to take a break and left. When he returned, there was a message from Mike. He called Mike and Mike told him to come to his office.

"Ed, you have two more complaints than the allowable amount. I've covered you to this point, but I can't anymore." Mike said.

"She's just a disgruntled client. She knew what she was getting into." Ed commented.

"Based on my conservation with her, I don't think so. I also spoke with her accountant. I can't stick my neck out anymore. I'm forced to terminate you."

"Surely, you're not serious. Look at the commissions I've generated. I've made a lot of money for this branch."

"Yes, and I appreciate that. But I have no other choice. I'm out on a limb and it's about to break."

"This isn't fair."

"Maybe not, but I have no other choice. I have rules to follow. You need to clean out your desk and leave."

"Go to hell."

Ed got his personal items out of his desk. As an after thought, he decided to take his book (client records). He then exited the building.

Mike checked his desk and noticed that the book was missing. He gave Ed time to get home and called him.

"Ed, this is Mike. I need your book back immediately."

"That's bullshit. It's my property because I opened the accounts."

"No, client records are the firms property. Read the broker manual."

"I'm keeping it."

"If it's not on my desk within two hours, I'm having you arrested for theft."

"You're a real asshole."

"Ed, I'm only trying to do my job. I wish you good luck in the future."

"If I interview with another firm and they call you, what will you say?"

"I'll tell them that you were a good producer."

"What about the complaints?

"That probably will not come up. Details of your complaints are on your license records and they'll already know about them."

"That sucks."

"Ed, you need to bring your book in."

"OK."

Ed came in and asked to see Mike. Mike's secretary said that he was in a meeting with some brokers and it may be a while. She said that he could give her his book. Ed said that he would handle it himself. He opened the door to Mike's office and threw the book on the floor. Then he left. Ed interviewed with several firms. When they got his complaint records, they decided to pass on him. Ed became a car salesman and did well at it. Since he had minimal repeat business, he could tell the customer what they wanted to hear and get away with it. He loved that.

Joe, regardless of Ed's problems, decided to trade more options. He pushed them with a vengeance. His commissions went up. As a result, he had a complaint within two weeks. He made the mandatory trip to Mike's office.

"Joe, you just received your second complaint." Mike said.

"What the hell for?" Joe asked.

"For not revealing the risks of option trading to a client."

"If they're so damn risky, why do we even trade them?"

"That's not the point. Some investors are more suitable to risk than others. You determine that by disclosing the risk and asking them if they're game."

"I don't think you can sell anything using that strategy."

"Yes you can. There are different strokes for different folks."

"I'll need to figure this one out."

"Joe, firm policy states that if you have four complaints, you are terminated. You have two. Watch what you say."

"I'll do that. Can I go back to work now?"

"Sure. Go out there and knock them dead."

After Joe left, Mike thought to himself that all the rules protecting the client were unjust. He felt that both the brokers and him could make much more money if these stupid rules were not in effect.

CHAPTER 8

John continued to do well with his strategy of catering to soon to be retired people and investing conservatively. In the meantime, he became a friend of Sam Stogler. Sam, like John, did not lie to clients and invested in a conservative manner. They went to lunch.

"Are we too honest for this business?" Sam asked.

John chuckled.

"I don't think so," John replied. "As long as we do what we're doing, we'll be OK."

"I hope so, but I'm thinking about getting out of this business."

"Why?"

"I'm growing weary of the constant pressure to generate commissions. Also, the lying and cheating going on around me bothers me."

"Sam, there's pressure in any job. You can't control the liars. If they're dishonest, you can't change them. They'll get their punishment. You can book on that."

"I don't know. Why do they keep getting away with it?"

"They don't. Ed got fired and Joe is in hot water."

"Yeah. I forgot about that. I still don't like the crap that goes on in this business."

"You can't change the world. It goes on in every business."

"How do you know?"

"Because I spent twenty years in the business world. This is your first job; so you don't know yet."

"Maybe I should find me a cabin in the woods and live off the land."

"That's probably good work if you can find it. I suggest that you look at other alternatives."

They both laughed.

When they returned to the office, John had a message from Mike. He needed to talk to John. He went to Mike's office.

"John, I want to congratulate you on your performance. But I have a way of improving it." Mike said.

"What's that?" John asked.

"You have a little over a million dollars in the money market fund. If you invest that, you'll reap huge commissions. That means that you'll fill up your pockets with money and the branch will benefit greatly."

"I can't."

"Why?"

"As you know, I cater to retirees. Most of them want to have funds in reserve for emergencies, such as medical problems. That's the reason that I have a large amount of money in the money market fund."

"John, do you realize how much money you can make by investing those funds?"

"Yes I do, but I'm not going to screw my clients for my own benefit."

"You're too idealistic. The name of this game is making money."

"That's possible, but I won't violate my principles."

"I understand that. However, you need to think about it."

"I will.

"You're a good man. Keep up the good work."

"Thanks, I will."

John left disgusted. When he returned to his desk, Joe approached him.

"Why were you in Mike's office?" Joe asked.

"He wants me to do more production." John replied.

"That's crazy. You're already in the top third of the office. What the hell is the deal?"

"Since I'm working with retirees, I have a large sum of money in the money market fund. He wants me to invest it."

"Why don't you?"

"Because they want a cash reserve."

"I see. Did you explain that to him?"

"Yes."

"What did he say?"

"He remained adamant that I consider investing it."

"Mike's an asshole. You're the most honest person I know. He's been on my back also."

"He's riding you because of complaints. Right?"

"I concede that."

"Joe, you need to clean up your act. If you don't, you'll not last in this business."

"I see what you're saying, but how do you sell anything without embellishing the benefits?"

"By being honest. You would be surprised by the number of people that appreciate that."

"John, you're proof of that. I'll try to do better."

"It'll pay off. Good luck with it."

"Thanks. I'll let you know how it goes."

Mike called Sam to his office.

"Sam, your production is not what it should be," Mike said.

"What should it be?" Sam asked.

"Approximately twice what it is now. Look at the standards."

"That goal will be difficult to achieve because I don't lie to clients like most of the brokers do. I have no complaints."

"There are some things you can do."

"What are they?"

"You have five hundred thousand in money markets. You should invest those funds. In addition, you need to move a good portion of your present investments into other investments."

"Both of those alternatives are unacceptable to both me and my clients."

"Sam, trust me, you need to do something in the near future. If you don't, your job will be in jeopardy."

"Thanks for the information. I'm going back to work."

"Good luck."

As Sam left, he decided to look for another job. John and he were regular lunch mates now. He walked by John's desk and told him that he had a story to tell at lunch. John smiled and said that he was sure he did because he had been to Mike's office.

At lunch, Sam was slightly depressed.

"What's wrong?" John asked.

"That asshole wants me to move my clients investments and also invest their cash reserves. Furthermore, he threatened me with my job if I didn't do it." Sam replied.

"That sounds like him."

"John, I've decided to get out of this screwed up business."

"What will you do?"

"I don't know, but I've been offered two jobs that I'm suitable for. It's been almost a month. I plan to pursue those first. If they don't work out, I'll look at other options."

"You'll land on your feet. Are we to remain fishing and hunting buddies?"

"You can count on that. You've taught me everything I know about those pursuits."

They returned to the office.

Sam immediately picked up the phone and called a company that offered him a job three weeks ago. This company specialized in designing pension plans for small firms that brokers cater to.

"Paul, this is Sam Stogler. Do you still need a good representative?" Sam asked.

"Yes. When can we get together?" Paul replied.

"I'm disgusted. I can come now."

"I'll see you in about thirty minutes."

Sam met with Paul. They negotiated a deal. Paul asked him when he could start. He said within three days. Paul told him to let him know when he was reporting.

Sam returned to the office, went to Mike's office, and told him that he had found another job and was resigning. He informed Mike that he had made arrangements to spend three days to make certain that the transition with his clients went smoothly.

"That's not necessary," Mike said. "I would prefer that you leave today."

"But I want to make sure that my clients are taken care of." Sam said.

"Don't worry about it. I'll take care of them."

"OK. Since my philosophy is the same as John's, I want him to have all my clients."

"That's not your call. I intend to hand them out to brokers that can earn commissions from them."

"They're not traders."

"They will be."

"Did anybody ever tell you that you don't give a damn about other people?"

Mike laughed.

"Yeah, my wife says the same thing. Sam, I'm a bottom line guy. People are secondary. They're tools of the trade. I didn't get to where I am by being nice to everyone."

"Mike, that attitude will eventually bring you down."

"Maybe so, but it's worked so far. You need to clean out your desk and go to your new job."

Sam left Mike's office and cleaned out his desk. He acquired a client list. He then visited John, told him the story, and said that he would call him tonight.

That evening, Sam called his clients. He explained the situation to them and told them to call Mike tomorrow and request John as their broker. He then informed them that if Mike would not cooperate, call the Regional Manager. He tried repeatedly to contact John. However,

John and his wife had gone out with friends and did not return home until very late.

The next morning, Mike's phone was constantly ringing because of calls from Sam's clients. He finally got a break in the calls and told his secretary to get John in his office. Mike was angry.

John, what the hell is going on?" Mike shouted.

"First of all, don't shout at me. Secondly, I don't know what you're talking about. What's the problem?" John asked.

"My phone has been ringing off the hook with calls from Sam's clients who want you to be their broker."

"That's the first time I've heard of it."

"Yeah, right. I believe that you and Sam colluded on this deal. You've dealt me a lot of grief. I think I'll fire you on the spot."

"Go ahead, but you will look very stupid firing one of your leading producers, who has no complaints."

"Get the hell out of my office. You'll not get one of Sam's accounts."

"Mike, I'm leaving your office. I really appreciate the support you demonstrate to your brokers."

John left wondering what was going on. He called the Regional Manager and told him that he felt as if he had been treated with disrespect. John was informed that this was not the first complaint and that he would address the issue.

That night, John called Sam. He related to Sam what happened and Sam told him what he did. John asked him why he did not let him know what was going on. Sam informed him that he tried but could not make contact.

The next day, Mike meted Sam's clients out to the brokers. John received none. The brokers were on the phone with Sam's clients immediately, looking for a quick sale. By noon, most of Sam's clients were on the phone to the Regional Manager. The Regional Manager called John. John told him what transpired. The manager told him that he did not have a problem with that and would call Mike. Kent Smith, the Regional Manager, called Mike.

"Mike, why am I getting all these calls from Sam's clients? Why can't you handle them yourself?" Kent asked.

"Sam and John colluded to transfer the accounts to John. That's a challenge to my authority. I'm pissed off." Mike replied.

"That's not what happened. I've spoken with both of them. John didn't know what was going on until he talked to Sam last night."

"They're liars."

"I don't believe so. I want you to call Sam's clients and ask them who they want their broker to be. Then assign them to that broker."

"Do you realize how long that will take?"

"I don't care. Would you prefer that they transfer their accounts to another firm?"

"No, I'll do it."

Mike made the calls. John got about two thirds of Sam's accounts. Mike was not happy. He felt that his authority had been questioned. He called John to his office.

"John, you've really done a number on me." Mike said.

"In what way?" John asked.

"By convincing Kent that Sam and you didn't collude."

"We didn't. I think you're paranoid."

"I don't believe that. I'll be watching you like a hawk."

"Mike, do what you need to do, but you're making a mistake."

"We'll see."

"It's a joy working with you."

John left.

CHAPTER 9

J oe and Cynthia were engaged in a torrid affair. They made love almost every night. Cynthia became pregnant. Joe was upset. He told Cynthia that they needed to have a conversation.

"I was under the impression that you were taking the pill," Joe said.

"I am. I must have missed a day," Cynthia replied.

"Great. The last thing I need is a kid. Get an abortion."

"Joe, I love you and want you to be the father of my child."

"I love you too, but get an abortion."

"I can't do that."

"Then what in the hell am I to do?"

"We could get married."

"I'm not responsible enough for that. I've always been a wild man."

"Yes, you're responsible enough. If we love each other, things will work out."

"I've got to think about this."

Joe left and went to a bar and got half drunk. In the bar, a young lady, Linda, approached him and stated that he acted depressed. She asked him what the problem was. He told her.

"What are you going to do about it?" Linda asked.

"I don't know. She wants to get married," Joe replied.

"What's wrong with that?"

"I don't think that I'm responsible enough for that."

"Do you love her?"

"Yeah."

"Then you're stupid not to marry her. Love happens rarely. I've been looking for it for a long time."

"I appreciate your time and advice. I need to get back and resolve this."

"Good luck."

Joe returned to his apartment. Cynthia had left. He then went to her apartment. She would not open the door. Joe shouted that if she did not open the door, he would kick it in. She opened it. Joe entered. She had tears in her eyes. Joe hugged her and told her that he loved her. She then started crying. Joe felt that he had hurt her. He hugged her again. He then said that he had an important announcement to make.

"What's that?" she asked.

"I don't really know how to go about this because I've never done it before. Hell, I'll just be blunt. I want you to be my wife," Joe said.

Cynthia was ecstatic. She started crying again. Joe told her that if she did not quit the crying, she would dehydrate and he did not want a dehydrated wife. She laughed. They decided to go to dinner to celebrate.

"Where do you want to go," Joe asked.

"I don't know. Maybe we can do Mexican food," Cynthia said.

"That's not good enough. Let's go to the Mansion."

"Joe, that's at least a two hundred dollar meal."

"Who gives a damn? You only have a beautiful woman accept your proposal once in life."

"Cynthia starts crying again and hugs Joe."

"Let's go."

"I can't yet. I need to freshen up my makeup and change clothes. Also, you need to put on a suit."

"Yeah, I forgot about that. That proves that I need a good wife. You get ready and we'll stop at my place so I can change clothes."

She finished her remake and they proceeded to Joe's apartment for clothes changing. Then they called for reservations and went to the Mansion.

They ordered their food. Joe added a nice vintage bottle of wine. Cynthia asked him if he knew how much the wine costs. He told her that he did not care because this was a special occasion. She laughed and said that she hoped that his production went up. They were both Catholic, so they would be married in that church. While they were eating, they struck up a conversation on where they would be married.

"Where do you want to get married?" Joe asked.

"I really don't have a preference. I guess your church or mine," Cynthia said.

"I have a really neat place in mind."

"Where's that?"

"Do you know where Rowlett is?"

"Yes, it's a suburb next to Lake Ray Hubbard."

"There's a very small wooden church there. It's been there for more than a hundred years. I think it would be appropriate because that's how long I want to be married to you."

Cynthia started laughing and had a problem stopping.

"What's the problem?" Joe asked.

"I think the expensive wine is affecting your mind. I've been hit on numerous times. I thought that I had heard every line. But yours is the best one yet. How can I turn that one down? We'll get married in the little church," Cynthia said.

"When?"

"It'll take about a month to get everything organized."

"I may back out by then. Let's do the deal in two weeks."

"You're a crazy person. OK, two weeks."

"Will this marriage last?"

"It must. Otherwise, I'll kill you."

Joe laughed and asked, "Am I marrying a mean woman?"

She chuckled and said, "Interpret it any way you want to."

"I think I'm in over my head."

"We'll see."

They smiled, got out of their seats, and hugged each other. Then they left.

The next day, Joe informed John of his engagement and told him that he worked fast because he already had an offspring in the works.

"Congratulations," John says. "But I have a question."

"What's that?" Joe asked.

"How did an ugly guy like you get hooked up with a good looking woman like Cynthia?"

"I have talent."

"You're talent must be world class."

They both laughed.

"John, you're the only person I know that's happily married," Joe says. "That may bring me good luck, so I want you to be my best man."

"It will be an honor."

"Thanks, the wedding is in about two weeks. I'll let you know the exact date this week."

"That's fine. Joe, you have responsibilities now. You need to change your attitude."

"I know. Will you help me?"

"You can count on it."

"I appreciate it. I'll talk to you later."

Joe decided to take the remainder of the day off to contemplate his future. He decided to be completely honest with his clients and to emulate John by leaning towards the conservative side.

The next day, Joe approached John's desk.

"Let's have lunch today. I'll spring for it." Joe said

"That's a sure winner," John replied.

They went to lunch.

"I've decided to change my act," Joe said. "But I need your help. I want to be honest and not risk much money. What are you doing?"

For the first time, John told another broker his strategy. He then requested that it be kept confidential.

"That's no problem. I think too much of you to break your trust. I don't think it'll work for me because you probably have a monopoly," Joe said.

"No, there's a long list of companies that have turned me down. Also, there's a lot that I haven't contacted. I have my hands full with the seminars I'm doing," John said.

"How do I pursue this?"

"I'll give you a list of the ones that turned me down. You know how it works. One broker can call and strike out and the next broker hits a home run."

"John, I really appreciate this."

"It's no big deal. Just treat Cynthia right."

"That's a guarantee."

They returned to the office. John gave him a list of the companies that turned him down. Joe spent the next three days calling them. He lined up several seminars. In the meantime, his production went down. Mike asked to see him.

"Joe, what's going on? You're commission level has gone to hell," Mike said.

"I've changed my philosophy. I've decided to be honest and treat my clients right," Joe stated.

"That's commendable, but what are going to do about your production?"

"It'll come."

"How?"

"I have several seminars lined up. It'll pay off."

"It better pay off, and in a hurry."

"Thanks for your support. I'm going back to work."

Joe asked John to help him with his first seminar. John agreed to do it. Joe thanked him and told him that the first one was next Monday night. John said that he would be there.

With John's help, the seminar went well. Joe opened two large accounts. He felt good because he did not lie to anyone.

The next day, he approached John.

"Why didn't you put me on this earlier?" Joe asked

"Because you've been a wild man. I didn't think you were ready for it," John replied.

"You're probably right."

"I think the pending marriage has had a positive affect on you."

"You're right again. It's made me reassess my life."

"That's good."

"Yeah, I'm a changed man."

"Lunch is on me today. You'll need the money when the baby comes."

Joe laughed and said, "I'm not financially destitute yet."

"But you will be."

"You're a jerk. I'm going back to work. And by the way, thanks for your help."

"I'm always willing to help out another jerk."

Joe smiled and left.

Joe had two more seminars during the week and did well at both. His production surged. Mike called him in.

"Joe, I'm proud of you. It requires a good broker to change their strategy and succeed," Mike said.

"Thanks," Joe said.

"If you move the money around a little, you can become a super star."

"I'll not do that. I already have two complaints and can't afford any more. Also, I'm investing in a conservative manner and it's not in the clients best interest to move the money."

"Are you turning into a John on me?"

"I presume so."

"I want you to think about that."

"I'll have all of next week to think about it because I'm taking off that week."

"Hell, why do you want to take off when you're on a roll?"

"Because I'm getting married this Saturday and I believe that a honeymoon is appropriate."

"I can't fault that. Good luck."

"Thanks."

Joe left and told John the wedding was at ten o'clock Saturday morning at the little Catholic Church in Rowlett. John asked for directions and Joe gave them to him. John then asked what time he should be there. Joe told him at nine thirty. Joe walked away, stopped and returned to John's desk.

He said that he almost forgot that there was a brief rehearsal Friday evening at six o'clock, followed by a rehearsal dinner at Culpepper Cattle Co. in Rockwall, which bordered Rowlett. John stated that he knew where it was because he had been there and that it is a nice place with good food.

The rehearsal went smoothly. Joe met Cynthia's parents for the first time. Her Father walked up to Joe.

"Will you take care of my daughter?" the Father asked.

"You can count on that. I wouldn't have married her if I didn't love her." Joe replied.

"Even under the circumstances?"

"Yes."

"At least you're an honest man. That's a rarity now."

"Don't worry about your daughter. She'll be treated extremely well."

"I appreciate that. Let's go get something to eat."

The group went to Culpepper Cattle Co. Cynthia sat down with an old friend, who would be her bridesmaid. The Father joined Joe. They had a long conversation. Joe learned that Cynthia's Dad is very wealthy. He owned a fifteen thousand acre ranch; complete with oil wells and cattle.

"How do you like the brokerage business," the Father asked.

"I enjoy it," Joe replied.

"Do you like to hunt?"

"Yes, that's one of my passions."

"Good, I have a proposition for you."

"What's that?"

"I make a lot of money from guided hunts on my ranch. I'm getting too damn old to oversee it. You can run it. I'll pay you more than you're making now. When can you start?"

"It's tempting, but I can't do it."

"Why."

"Because I don't want to be a kept man."

"You're looking at it the wrong way. You'll be family."

"Why are you offering me this?"

"I'm not getting any younger. Cynthia is my only child. I want her near me and I want to watch my grandchildren have fun on the ranch. I also need to show a man how to run the ranch because Cynthia will inherit it. She's too kind to run an operation as large as mine."

"I see where you're coming from. You have me wavering a little. However, I need to put some deep thought into this and to talk to Cynthia about it."

"That's fine."

After the dinner, Cynthia and Joe were driving back to Dallas.

"I didn't know that I was marrying money," Joe said.

"That's a bonus that I didn't tell you about. Are you going to back out because I'm a little rich girl?" Cynthia asked.

"Should I."

"If you do, I'll have you killed."

"OK, the wedding will take place."

"That's decent of you."

"Your Dad offered me a job."

"I suspected that. Let me guess. He wants you to learn how to run the ranch."

"Yeah, what do you think?"

"I don't know. You'll eventually need to do it. I'm not sure I want to do it now. I'm inclined to stay in Dallas for a while. What do you think?"

"I have mixed emotions. I need to think about it. I'll do whatever you want to do."

"Does that mean that I'm in control of the decisions?"

"Hell no. But it is your family. I want to give you a voice in the decision making."

They arrived at Cynthia's apartment. She told him to come in for a drink. He replied that he could not because the wedding was tomorrow and the good things must be saved until the honeymoon. She laughed and kissed him goodnight.

John arrived an hour and fifteen minutes early for the wedding. As he parked, Joe drove up.

"What do we do now?" John asked.

"We need to go to the Priest's chambers and go over last minute details," Joe said.

When they were with the priest, he related what would happen. He then discussed the ring ceremony. Joe panicked. He stated that he had forgotten the ring and that Cynthia would kill him. Both the Priest and John laughed and made disparaging remarks about Joe's memory.

"Guys, this not funny. I'm about to mess up my wedding," Joe said.

"Give me your key," John said. "I'll retrieve the ring. Where is it?"

"In the far right drawer of the dresser in my bedroom."

"What's it in?"

"A small velvet covered case."

"Father, I may be little late getting back."

"Don't worry about it. I'll handle it."

John left. As he was getting into his car, he realized that he would be very late because Joe lived in Plano. He remembered that the police station was only about four hundred yards down the street. He surmised that anything was worth a try. He pulled into the station and went in. He asked to see an officer. A detective came out. He looked at John's tux and asked him if he is getting married in the station.

"No, I have a problem," John said.

"What is it?" the detective asked.

John explained the situation and asked if he could get an escort to Joe's apartment.

"This is the weirdest request I've ever had. Jim, do we have a squad car available?" the detective yelled.

"Yeah" Jim said

"Bring me the keys."

They walked out of the station.

"Should I follow you?" John asked.

"Hell no. That bullshit is for TV and the movies. It's better to have one person driving crazy than two. Get into the squad car," the detective replied.

John gave him directions. The detective decided to take 190 to Plano. When they cleared traffic, he turned on the lights and proceeded at a rapid pace. John attempted to strike up a conversation.

"Don't break my concentration. Otherwise, we'll both be dead," The detective said.

They drove to Joe's place in silence. John retrieved the ring. He noticed a bottle of unopened Jack Daniel bourbon on the kitchen cabinet.

"Do you drink bourbon?" John asked.

"Sure," The detective answered.

John handed him the bottle.

"This is on the groom."

"Thanks. He's a generous man."

They arrived at the church five minutes before the start of the wedding. John thanked the detective, gave him his card, and told him that dinner for him and his wife was free. He then informed him to call when he could go.

John rushed to the Priest's office. Joe breathed a sigh of relief.

"I couldn't find it," John said. "I looked in every drawer. We'll wing it. You can put my ring on her finger. Nobody will ever know."

Joe broke into a sweat.

"She'll know," Joe said. "It'll destroy my marriage. Father, can we postpone the wedding?"

"That's an unusual request. That will do more harm than the lack of a ring.," The Priest said.

John pulled out the ring case. Joe broke into a big smile. The Priest and John roared with laughter.

"Father, can I curse in front of you?" Joe asked.

"Only once," he replied.

"John, you're an asshole. I'll get even."

"Let's get on with the show," the Priest said.

The entire branch was invited. All but a few showed up. The wedding went smoothly. Cynthia's Dad had made arrangements for the reception to be held at the Anatole in Dallas. The crowd went there.

Expensive bottles of bourbon and other liquor was behind the catered bar and expensive champagne on ice was prevalent. In addition, bits of lobster, crab legs, and caviar were plentiful. The participants attacked both the bar and the finger food. Everybody had a good time.

After the reception, the newly weds flew to Tobago, a small Caribbean island, for their honeymoon.

CHAPTER 10

Joe and Cynthia returned from the honeymoon. They went to the office on Monday. Mike called Joe in.

"Joe, how did it go?" Mike asked.

"It went great," Joe replied.

"Good. But this has set your production far back. You need to make up for it."

"Mike, what the hell is going on? A person can't get married without having pressure for production put on them?"

"Commissions are the name of the game."

"I'll do the best I can. That's all I can do."

"I appreciate your positive attitude."

Joe left and went to John's desk. He told John about the conversation.

"What should I do?" Joe asked.

"Call Kent. I think he's about fed up with Mike," John answered.

"I'll do it and let you know what happens."

Joe called Kent.

"Kent, this is Joe Dunigan. I have a problem I need to talk to you about." Joe said.

"I know who you are, Joe. You're in the top half of production in your office," Kent said.

Joe related his conversation with Mike.

"That's bullshit," Kent said. "I'll take care of it."

Joe returned to John's desk and told him what transpired. John stated that another nail in Mike's coffin was in place. Joe said that he needed advice on another subject.

"You know me," John said. "I'm always ready to mete out advice."

"My father-in-law offered me a job," Joe said.

"Doing what?"

"He wants me to learn how to run his ranching operations."

"Why?"

"Cynthia is an only child. He thinks that a woman's place is in the home. Also, Cynthia doesn't want to run it."

"Is he wealthy?"

"Yes, very. The first I knew of it was at the rehearsal. During this entire ordeal, Cynthia never mentioned it. That shows character."

"You're right. You're lucky to have her. My advice is based on a time tested Texas truth. Don't look a gift horse in the mouth."

"I'll be a kept man."

"I don't think so. You'll be more like family. After all, he's grooming you to inherit the ranch. Talk to Cynthia about it and make a joint decision."

Joe left. Cynthia walked up.

"What did you advise him to do?" she asked.

"I told him that it's a decision for the two of you to make jointly," John said.

"What should I do?"

"You only have two choices. If you want to keep the ranch in the family, you must do what your Dad is proposing. Otherwise, you'll have to sell it when your parents die because nobody will know how to run it."

"That's good advice. It narrows the choices. However, I want to hang around in Dallas for a while."

"That's fine, but if you want the ranch, you need to make a decision soon. You never know what the future will bring."

"I know. Thanks for your time."

Cynthia had a lot on her mind. The pregnancy and the ranch decision were distracting her. As a result, her production was going down. Prior to this, she had been a top producer. Mike summoned her to his office.

"Cynthia, your production is down dramatically. What's the problem?" Mike asked.

"With my new situation, I have a lot on my mind. I'm having a problem concentrating," Cynthia replied.

"Have you lost interest?"

"No."

"Can you turn it around?"

"Yes, with time."

"Cynthia, you don't have much time. The amount of overhead we have to support brokers does not justify low achievers."

"Have I been a low achiever?"

"No, but present performance is what determines the bottom line."

"So you'll not give me time to sort this out?"

"I don't have time. A large portion of my compensation is based on the monthly profitability of the branch."

"Mike, are you telling me that you will not give up a little to help a top producer who has made you money?"

"I can't. I have commitments."

"I do too."

She walked out.

John continued to do well. He was now the leading producer in the branch.

That night, Cynthia told Joe what transpired with Mike.

"I'll talk with the asshole tomorrow," Joe said.

"No, don't give him the pleasure," Cynthia said.

"What I have to say will not be pleasurable to him."

"Please don't. Let me handle it."

"OK."

Cynthia's production continued to plummet. Mike called her in and fired her. She told Joe that she had been fired. He was furious.

"Are you ready to move to the ranch?" he asked.

"Yes," Cynthia answered.

"Good. We'll have to after my conversation with Mike."

He stormed into Mike's office.

"Mike, if you were not such a wimp, I'd whip your ass right now," Joe said.

"You're not man enough," Mike replied.

"Then let's find out."

"No, that's stupid."

"That proves you're a wimp."

"Joe, I did what I had to do. It's no reflection on you. In fact, I want you to remain with the firm."

"In your dreams. You can take this job and shove it where the sun doesn't shine. I quit."

Joe left angry. He told Cynthia that they needed to clean out their desks. She asked him if he quit. He replied that he had quit. They went to John's desk to say goodbye. Mike came by.

"You two need to leave the office," Mike said.

"Go to hell," Joe replied. "I'll leave whenever I'm ready."

"Then I'm forced to call the police."

"Do it. That'll give me an excuse to sue you. I'm a client now. I'm talking to my broker."

Mike's face turned red and he returned to his office.

"I regret that you two are leaving," John said. "But I know the circumstances and wish you the best of luck."

"We appreciate that," Joe said.

"John, we'll miss you," Cynthia said. "Will you and your family visit us at the ranch?"

"You can count on it," John said.

Before Joe left, he called Kent.

"Kent, how are you?" Joe asked.

"Good. What's going on?" Kent asked.

Joe told him what happened.

"Tell Cynthia not to leave. I'll be there within thirty minutes."

"It's too late. I've already quit and we have other things to pursue."

"Will you give me a chance to talk you out of it?"

"I respect you, but I have made a decision."

"Are you sure?"

"Yes."

"If it's any consolation, I'm getting rid of Mike as soon as possible."

"I think that's a wise move."

"Joe, good luck to you."

"Thanks,"

They hung up. Cynthia and Joe left the premises.

Kent called John.

"John, I need to talk to you. Come downtown," Kent said.

"What do you need to talk to me about?" John asked.

"I'll tell you when you get here."

"What time?"

"Now."

"I'm on my way."

"OK."

John entered Kent's office.

"What's this all about?" John asked.

"John, I've looked at your background. You have a lot of management experience. In addition, you have a reputation as a clean broker. I intend to fire Mike as soon as possible. His turnover is much too high and his attitude stinks. I want you to manage the branch effective tomorrow," Kent said.

"I don't think you want me to manage the branch."

"Why?"

"I know too much. There are a lot of brokers that lie and cheat their clients. I don't think they deserve to be in the business. Mike condones it if they're good producers. I'd fire half the brokers the first day."

"You're right about one thing. We can't afford to lose half the brokers in one day."

"Kent, that proves I'm not a candidate."

"No, it doesn't. I respect your ethics. I need a favor."

"What is it?"

"I want you to manage the branch for a week or two to enable me to find a manager. But please don't fire anybody without checking with me."

"I'll do that deal."

"Good. Let's go to the branch so I can remove this thorn from my side."

John beat Kent to the branch and went to his desk. Kent entered shortly thereafter and entered Mike's office.

"Mike, I'm forced to terminate you," Kent said.

"Why? I have a profitable branch," Mike said.

"You'll not have a profit for long. I'm getting too many broker complaints and your turnover rate is not acceptable."

"What the hell do you want me to do? Handle them with kid gloves?"

"No, you should have handled them as humans."

"You're full of crap."

"That's possible, but I want you to clean out your personal items while I observe and leave."

Mike got his briefcase. The first thing he pulled out of his desk was a list of the branch's clients.

"Put that back. That's not your personal property." Kent said.

Mike returned it to his desk and retrieved his personal things. Then he left.

Kent called a meeting. He informed the brokers that Mike was no longer with the firm and that John would be the interim manager until he could find a permanent replacement.

"Why don't you make John permanent," one of the brokers asked. "He'll be a good manager."

"Because he doesn't want the job," Kent replied. "He's doing me a favor by filling in. Now, I'll let John say a few words."

"I don't know how long I'll be the manager. However, in the meantime, I'll have some expectations. First of all, work hard. Secondly, be honest with your clients. That includes disclosing risk. If I observe otherwise, or get a complaint in that area, I will deal with it harshly. If you do your job and observe those rules, I work for you. You don't work for me," John said.

The meeting ended. Kent told John that he did a good job and left.

CHAPTER 11

Joe and Cynthia arrived at the ranch. They turned left on a gravel road and proceeded about a mile to the ranch house. As they approached the house, Joe was amazed. It was a three story, sprawling mansion.

"Hell, I've seen hotels smaller than this," Joe said.

Cynthia laughed.

"It's a nice house," she said. "Some day, it will be ours."

"I'm in awe."

"Don't be. You'll get accustomed to it."

They walked to the front door. Cynthia's Dad met them with a big smile on his face.

"Welcome to the ranch," he said.

"It's good to be here, Mr. Arnold," Joe replied.

"Forget that Mister stuff. You're family now. Call me Clint."

"I will."

"Where's Mama?" Cynthia asked.

"She went to town to tell the caterer to get on the move because we're having a Texas style cookout tonight. All of the ranch hands are invited. I want them to meet Joe."

"I'll go get the stuff out of the car and trailer," Joe said.

"Forget it. I'll have the help do it," Clint replied.

"That's fine with me."

Clint said that he needed to talk with them in the library. They entered the library. There were more books than a person could read in a lifetime.

"You have two choices," Clint said. "You can live in this house and have the entire third floor, or we can build you a nice house on the other side of the ranch. That'll give you more privacy. Which do you prefer?"

"Can we discuss it in private?" Cynthia asked.

"Sure, but don't take long to make a decision. In the meantime, you can have the third floor."

"Clint, I appreciate your generosity," Joe said.

"No problem. You married my daughter. But I do have a change in plans for you."

"What is it?"

"We originally talked about you running the hunting operation. However, my ranch manager quit last week to return to his family ranch. That means that you are now the ranch manager. I'll give you a crash course on what to do. In addition, you'll spend all day with my ranch foreman for a period of time. Is that OK with you?"

"Yes."

"I'm prepared to offer you a hundred thousand a year. Is that acceptable?"

"Clint, that's more than generous."

"As I said, you're family now."

"I will not let you down."

"I know that. I'm a good judge of character. Let's unload your stuff and move you upstairs."

They went to the front of the house. All their goods were on the floor and there were three ranch hands standing around to help.

"Clint, Where are the stairs? I'll help them," Joe said.

"Turn right at the second hallway and go to the end. Forget the stairs. There's an elevator as you enter the hallway. Get situated and be at the pavilion at six o'clock. The cook out will start then." Clint said.

"We'll be there."

Cynthia and Joe went to the third floor. It had everything a normal house did, including a kitchen, living room, den, and three bedrooms.

"Where do you want to live?" Joe asked.

"I'd prefer to live here. There are benefits. We'll have maid service. Also, Mama has a cook. That means I can ride my horses and lead a life of ease. And I don't want Daddy to pay for building us a house." Cynthia said.

"We can build it ourselves."

"You don't know him. He'll not let you."

"Then I presume a decision has been made."

"Yes."

At six o'clock, they went to the cookout. There were about a hundred people present. The caterer had cooked approximately one hundred and twenty-five pounds of meat, consisting of brisket, ribs, sausage, and chicken. Vegetables were also bountiful. Two kegs of beer added to the festivities.

Clint walked up to Joe.

"I think it would be wise to mingle and meet the ranch hands, but first I want you to meet the ranch foreman, Juan Perez," Clint said.

Clint motioned to Juan. Juan came over.

"Juan, this is my new son-in-law and ranch manager, Joe Dunigan. I would like for you to train him. Is that OK?"

"It'll be a pleasure." Juan said.

"I'll give Joe a tour of the ranch tomorrow. After that, he's all yours."

"No problem."

"Thanks."

Juan said that he was going to the nearest beer keg. Clint told Joe that they needed to follow Juan. Joe got a beer and mingled with the ranch hands. He soon discovered that about a third of them barely spoke English. He decided that he needed to learn Spanish.

The food was plentiful and the appetites were large. Everyone had a feast. A large quantity of food was left over. The ranch hands bagged up what they wanted and took it home.

Clint and Mary, his wife, and Cynthia and Joe walked back to the house. On the way, Clint informed Joe that they would tour the ranch at first light. Breakfast would be at five thirty AM.

Cynthia and Joe went upstairs.

"Set the alarm at 4:30," Joe said. "Do you want to get up at that ungodly hour to eat breakfast at 5:30?"

"Certainly, that's the time we eat breakfast every morning. You rise early when you're a rancher," Cynthia said.

"That's great."

"You'll adjust to it."

At daylight the next morning, Clint and Joe boarded a pickup truck and began the tour. They drove on dirt roads. Joe noticed there were numerous oil wells pumping.

"You have a lot of oil wells," Joe said.

"Yeah, that's how I make most of my money. Sooner or later, they'll all run dry. But you don't need to worry about it. I've set up a trust fund of a few million for Cynthia. That will enable you two to keep the ranch and thrive. However, you'll need to come up with other ways to generate income so your kids can do well when you die," Clint said.

"You obviously plan ahead."

"I try to. Since we're talking business, I'll fill you in on the cattle operation. The cows are a pain in the ass. It's a breakeven proposition. One year you'll make a little and the next you'll lose some. Also, it's a real problem finding them all at roundup time. Because of the hassle, I only run about a thousand head."

"If they're not profitable, why do you keep them?"

"I like to watch them. Plus that, who as ever heard of a ranch without cattle and cowboys? Look what we have here."

There was a large rattlesnake crossing the road. Clint sped up, aimed a tire at the snake, and slammed on his brakes. He backed up. The snake was dead. He exited the truck and cut off the rattlers. He handed them to Joe and stated that he had a souvenir to show his city friends.

"Are there many of them around here?" Joe asked.

"They're everywhere."

"How do you avoid them?"

"You don't. You wear snake proof boots."

"That makes sense."

Joe noticed a buck deer. His rack looked huge. He asked Clint to stop the truck. Clint reached into the back of the truck and gave binoculars to Joe. He is amazed by the size of the buck.

"Clint, that's the largest buck I've seen." Joe said.

"This is the first time I've seen him. He's definitely Boone and Crocket Club caliber. You need to know that the hunting operation is a big money maker. We've had a lot of Boone and Crocket bucks killed on this ranch," Clint stated.

"I believe it."

They continued to tour the ranch. After four and a half hours, Clint said that they needed to go back for lunch.

"You told me that you had fifteen thousand acres. It's obviously much larger than that," Joe said.

Clint laughed.

"I didn't want to intimidate you," Clint said. "I was afraid that you wouldn't come work for me. I own twenty thousand acres and lease fifteen thousand acres on the west side."

Clint spotted a wild hog with three young hogs in tow.

"How far do you think they are?" Clint asked.

"About a hundred and fifty yards," Joe replied.

Clint reached into the crew cab and pulled out a .270 caliber rifle.

"Shoot one of the young ones. We'll smoke it for supper," Clint said.

Joe got out of the truck and rested the rifle on the hood of the truck. Then he asked Clint at what range the rifle was sighted in. Clint told him a hundred yards. The hogs saw Joe and ran. One of the young ones was curious and stopped to look at Joe. He held high behind the shoulder and squeezed off a shot. The pig collapsed.

"That was a hell of a shot," Clint said.

"Thanks," Joe replied.

Clint opened the glove compartment and retrieved a knife. He put up the .270 and got a shotgun. He then informed Joe that he could gut the pig.

"What's the shotgun for," Joe asked.

"Since you don't have on snake proof boots, I'll run interference for you," Clint answered.

"I'll buy that."

Joe gutted the pig and threw it into the back of the truck. They then headed for the house for lunch.

Clint summoned Juan and instructed him to have a ranch hand finish dressing the pig and smoke it.

The next morning at daylight, Joe met Juan. Juan informed him that today, he would learn where the oil tanks were and how to load the tankers that picked it up. Also, he would learn where all the deer stands were located. They left in Juan's pickup truck.

"I'm very happy that you're here," Juan said.

"Why?" Joe asked.

"Because if Cynthia had not found a husband that was willing to come here, she would have sold the ranch. I don't want to leave here because I'm very happy on this ranch."

"As long as I'm alive, you'll not leave."

Juan broke into a big smile.

"Juan, I need to learn Spanish. Will you teach me?"

"Sure. First, you'll learn the vocabulary. Then we'll get into the verbs and sentence structure."

"You sound educated. Do you have a degree?"

"Yes, in ranch management from Texas A&M."

"You'll be the next ranch manager."

"Thanks, but I've turned it down twice."

"Why?"

"I didn't want the hassle."

"Would you consider it?"

"Maybe."

Juan turned at a one-lane dirt road.

"Where are we going?" Joe asked.

"To a deer stand. All of the one lane roads go to a stand," Juan said.

They arrived at the stand. It was approximately twenty feet high. It was roofed and had enclosed sides. The sides had large slots from which to shoot. They climbed the ladder and entered the stand. It had chairs and a sofa.

"When the season starts, we put a Coleman stove in here to enable them to cook their lunch if they want to," Juan said. "When it gets cold, we put in Coleman heaters. For some damn reason, the hunters want semi luxury."

Juan showed Joe the remainder of the deer stands. By this time, it was noon.

"Are we going to the house for lunch?" Joe asked.

"No, when you're working, that takes up too much time," Juan replied.

Juan pulled a cooler from the crew cab of the truck. There was lunch in it.

Juan toured the oil tanks and showed Joe what to do. This took the remainder of the afternoon.

In about thirty days, Joe spoke Spanish reasonably well and had learned most of the inner aspects of the ranch.

CHAPTER 12

John spent the first few days learning company policies and the inner workings of the office. Then he called in Sue, the mutual fund switcher.

"Sue, we have a minor problem," John said.

"What's that?" Sue asked.

"I want you to stop switching funds unless there is a compelling reason."

"I always have a good reason."

"I know better. I spent time with you."

"Look, I have only two complaints and I'm generating large commissions."

"Two complaints are too many for a broker pushing mutual funds."

"OK, I'll do what you say, but my production will go down."

"That's acceptable as long as you maintain a reasonable level of production."

"I do appreciate that."

She returned to her desk.

Next, John called in Jim, the short-term stock trader.

"Jim, how's it going?" John asked.

"It's going well. I'm having a good month." Jim said.

"I need a favor."

"What is it?"

"I don't mind you trading stocks because a lot of people like to do it. But I want you to quit lying to them. You already have three complaints. One more and you're out of the business."

"Yeah, I know. I need to clean up my act."

"That's a good attitude. There are often valid reasons to switch to another stock. If you get a complaint under those circumstances, it'll be thrown out."

"Thanks for the advice."

John toured the office and mingled with the brokers. Two of them told him that they needed to talk to him as soon as possible. He informed them to give him ten minutes to finish his tour and come to his office. The two brokers were Corey and James. They entered John's office.

"What's going on guys?" John asked.

"We have a serious problem," Corey said.

"What is it?"

"Sue is stealing leads from other brokers," James replied.

"That's a serious accusation." John said. "Do you have proof?"

Both of them produced four or five lead cards. They pointed out that the initial handwriting was theirs and the subsequent writing was Sue's.

"Where did you find these?" John asked.

"We stayed late yesterday and went through her lead file," Corey replied. We've suspected her for a long time. I once called a prospect that I had two cards on and she told me that Sue was her broker."

"There are numerous cards in her file with multiple handwriting," James said.

"I want you to keep this quiet," John said. "I don't want her to get wind of it. I'll go through her card file tonight to confirm your concern. Then I'll fire her when she comes in tomorrow."

"Why don't you sign on as the permanent manager?" Corey asked. "You're the best manager we've had."

"I don't know if I want to," John replied. "I hate to fire people. In this business, you're firing them too often."

"Think about it," James said.

"I will," John replied. "And by the way, I appreciate the efforts of both of you. You're honest brokers and do decent production."

They said thanks and left.

John stayed late and waited for Sue to leave. At seven o'clock, she was still there. The late shift was apparently when she did her mischief. She finally gave up and went home. John checked her lead file. There were many cards with more than one person's handwriting on them. He gathered the cards and her client records. Then he put her personal items in a sack. He called Kent at home and related the situation.

"I've been in this business for twenty years," Kent said. This is the most despicable thing I've heard of. Get her stuff out of her desk and fire her when she comes in tomorrow."

"I already have the stuff. I'll carry out the remainder of the task in the morning," John said.

"You're a good man."

"I apologize for bothering you at home."

"No problem. This had to be dealt with immediately."

The next morning, John intercepted Sue as she entered the branch and escorted her to his office.

"What's going on?" Sue asked.

"You've been stealing leads from other brokers," John replied.

"That's bullshit. Who told you that?"

"Other brokers."

"They're lying."

"I don't think so. I have hard evidence."

"Like what?"

John explained to her what he found going through her card files.

"Oh, that explains it. Those leads were given to me by other brokers that couldn't do anything with them."

"I'm not buying that. Brokers have found their leads in your file."

"They're after me because I'm a woman."

"Sue, there are many female brokers in this office. None of them have been accused of anything. Here are your personal things. Your employment has ended. I'll escort you to the door."

"You can't do this. I'm calling Kent and getting you fired."

"That's your privilege, but he has already approved it."

"Then I'm suing for sexual harassment and defamation of character."

"That's your right. However, the only people that will make money are your attorneys."

"You're a real son-of-a-bitch."

"I've been called worse. I need your office key."

"I'm keeping it."

"Do I need to call the police to retrieve it?"

She reached into her purse and threw the key at him. He escorted her out of the office.

John called a meeting of the brokers. He told them that a broker had been terminated for borrowing leads from other brokers. This drew a laugh.

"I'll read the names from the cards," John said. "If it's yours, raise your hand and I'll pass it to you."

John read the names and distributed the cards. He then passed out the unclaimed leads. The meeting adjourned. As they were leaving, two of the brokers approached John and told him that they respected him for his actions.

"Thanks," John said.

"This is not a new problem," one broker said. "Mike knew about it but said he couldn't prove it."

"While I'm the manager, I'll support the brokers," John said.

"Why don't you sign on for the long term?" the other broker asked.

"I'm not sure I want to."

"The brokers in the branch would be happy if you did."

"I appreciate your support. I'll think about it."

As John was returning to his office, he noticed that Kent was mingling with the brokers. He wondered what was going on but did not really care. He entered his office and made calls to his clients. Kent walked in.

"Hi Kent. What's happening?" John asked.

"You're the main show. You're doing an excellent job. I've visited with the brokers and almost all of them respect you," Kent said.

"That's good news."

"John, I want you to be the branch manager. I'll not take no for an answer. I have a solution for weeding out the bad actors. You can do it gradually at your discretion. We can't do it all at once because of the loss of revenues. In the meantime, I'll send you all the trainees you want. In addition, you can recruit brokers from other firms. I'll provide reasonable bonus money for them. Does that make sense?"

"Yes, but I need to sleep on it."

"Does that mean that you'll have a decision tomorrow?"

"Yes."

"OK, I'll talk to you tomorrow."

John talked to his wife, Betty, when he got home.

"What do you think?" John asked.

"It's your decision. You know me. I never give you advice on your career. You'll have to live with your own decision," Betty said.

"Wow, you're a big help."

John had trouble sleeping. He got up several times. He was having difficulty making a decision.

The next morning, Betty asked him what he decided.

"Nothing," John said. "I'll decide on the way to work."

"Good luck." Betty said.

"Thanks."

When John arrived at the office, Kent was waiting for him.

"What did you decide?" Kent asked.

"I'll do it if the money is right," John answered.

"You'll have a base salary of a hundred and fifty thousand. That's slightly more than you're making now. In addition, I'll give you fifteen percent of the branch profits. That means that the job should be worth two hundred thousand plus. Is that acceptable?"

"I can live with that."

"Call a meeting and I'll make the announcement."

The brokers gathered in the meeting room.

"John is your new branch manager," Kent said. "He has many years of management experience. I've talked with most of his superiors and they praised him. They said that he is not only efficient; he is also fair and has principles. Those are characteristics that are needed in this business. John, do you have anything to say?"

"No. By now, I think that everybody knows how I operate," John replied.

The meeting broke up. Kent shook hands with John and told him that the show was now all his. Kent then left.

John had three relatively new brokers that were below standard on their production. They have had no complaints. Instead of firing them, he decided to try to help them. He called in Keith first.

"Keith, you're below standard. What can I do to help?" John asked.

"Are you calling me in to fire me?" Keith asked.

"No, I'm here to help you."

"I don't know what the problem is. I call all of my clients that I can get a hold of every day. I want to service them so that they'll give me more business."

"I believe you just revealed the problem."

"Tell me what it is."

"You have only about a hundred clients. You need three or four times that many. How many prospecting calls do you make a day?"

"About ten."

"That's the problem. You need to make twenty or thirty to enable you to get your client base up. Calling your clients every day is a waste of time. They don't demand that. In fact, it may irritate some of them."

"When should I call them?"

"When there's a reason, such as a development in their investment or when you want to sell them something that you think they'll be interested in. Remember, you need to know your client. By that, I mean know their financial status and their attitude about different investments."

"How do you find that out?"

"By asking. They'll respect you for your interest."

"You've taught me something today."

"That's great. Get out there and try it."

Keith left full of enthusiasm. John next called in Lucinda.

"Lucinda, your production is not what it should be. Is there a reason?" John asked.

"I'm not a trader. I'm trying to be conservative by pursuing retirees," Lucinda replied.

"How are you going about it?"

"I call human resource managers and ask them to call me when someone is retiring."

"How many calls have you gotten?"

"Very few."

"You're doing it wrong. I built my book by catering to the same market segment. You must offer a service. When I called human resources, I told them that I'm offering free seminars at their business for people that are retiring within the year. You know what the results were."

"That is so logical that it's scary. I'll do it."

"Good luck."

John next called in Jose.

"I know why I'm here," Jose said. "My production is low. In addition to that, I hate this business. I'm resigning now."

"Jose, you don't need to do that. I'll help you," John said.

"I made up my mind about this two weeks ago."

"Jose, I wish you the best."

"I know that you're a sincere person. I thank you for that. I have a tentative job offer. If they call you, will you give me a good reference?"

"You can count on it."

"Thanks. I'll get my stuff and leave."

CHAPTER 13

Monday morning, Karen, his secretary, informed John that he had a call from the Dallas Police Department. John wondered which broker got drunk this weekend. He picked up the phone.

"Mr. Simpson, this is Sgt. Gonzales."

"What can I do for you Sergeant?" John asked.

"Your wife has been in an automobile accident."

"Is it serious?"

"Yes, she's at Parkland Hospital."

"Were my boys involved?"

"No, they're at school."

"Thanks for calling."

Since Parkland had one of the best trauma units in the country, John knew that it was bad. He called the school and told them that Karen was picking up his boys. He told Karen to let Kent know that he would be out of the office and to pick up the boys and bring them to Parkland.

He rushed to Parkland and entered the emergency room. He requested to see his wife. He was told that the doctors were working on her and he could not go in. He sat down in the lounge. He was a platoon leader in the Army. He reflected that this was worse than combat.

There were several people in the lounge. Nobody was talking. Suddenly, one of the women started crying and flailing her arms. John went over to comfort her.

"What's wrong?" John asked.

"My son shot himself. It must be my fault," She replied.

"No it's not. If you blame everything in life on yourself, you'll be miserable. People make their own choices."

She calmed down and thanked him for his support. He returned to his seat. Karen brought in his sons, Randy and Eric. Randy was twelve and Eric fourteen. They sat down next to him. Karen said that she would like to stay. John stated that she could.

"Daddy, what's wrong with Mama?" Randy asked.

"She was in a bad car wreck," John answered.

"Will she make it?" Eric asked.

"I don't know Son."

They sat in silence for approximately two hours. Finally, a doctor came out. He noticed that the boys were present and asked to see John in private.

"What's the prognosis?" John asked.

"We did all we could. Unfortunately, your wife is brain dead. We have her on life support so you can see her before we disconnect. Do you want to see her?" the doctor asked.

"Yes."

"I'll take you to her."

John entered the room and looked at her. For the first time since his Sergeant was killed in combat, he cried. He left to inform his boys.

"Guys, the news I have is not good," John said. "Your mother didn't make it."

John began crying again. Both of the boys also cried. John hugged them. Karen also hugged them.

"Dad, why did this happen?" Randy asked.

"I don't know Son. Sometimes, bad things happen in life. We'll miss your Mother, but we must go about living our lives," John replied.

John thanked Karen for her support and took the boys home. He immediately made arrangements for a Thursday funeral and called her family. He then made arrangements for a sitter to pick the boys up at school and watch them until he got home. He called Kent.

"Kent, this is John. My wife died. I need to take the rest of the week off."

"Karen has already called. John, my heart goes out to you. Take as much time as you need. Do you have someone in mind to run the branch or do you want me to run it?" Kent said.

"Nick Moore can run it. He's a big producer and is honest. The other brokers respect him."

"I'll call him now. If there's anything I can do, let me know."

"Thanks Kent."

Karen called Joe at the ranch.

"Joe, this is Karen. John's wife was killed in an automobile accident today."

"You're kidding," Joe said.

"I wish that I was."

"I'll be there tomorrow. Thanks for calling."

The next day, Cynthia and Joe checked into the Anatole and went to John's house.

"John, I don't know what to say. I'm sorry about this," Joe said.

"Bad things sometimes happen," John said.

They visited for about an hour. After that, Joe had a proposal.

"John, I have a proposition," Joe said.

"Give it to me," John said.

"After the funeral, bring the boys to the ranch for a couple of days. They can ride horses and have fun. Also, we'll tour the ranch and let them see deer, turkeys, and hogs. It'll help get their minds off the adversity."

"That sounds good. I'll take you up on it."

John asked Joe to be a pallbearer and he agreed.

Terri Crowle, John's former sales assistant, had cooked a turkey, complete with dressing and vegetables. She took it to John's house. John answered the door and invited her in. He then thanked her for the food. They hugged.

"I'll leave now," Terri said. "I know that you need privacy."

"No, don't leave. Cynthia and Joe are here. You can visit with old friends," John said.

They went to the living room.

"Terri, you get better looking every day," Joe said.

"If you're that generous, I should have tried for you," she replied. "But Cynthia beat me to the punch."

Everybody laughed.

"Terri, have you found Mr. Perfect yet?" Cynthia asked.

"No, but I'm searching like hell," Terri said.

Terri asked about the ranch. They described it to her and invited her to visit them.

"I'll do it. I'm a cowgirl at heart," Terri said.

At approximately four o'clock, Kent and Karen arrived at almost the same time with more food. He invited them in. Kent said he had a meeting and must leave. Karen came in. She visited with Cynthia and Joe.

At five o'clock, John announced that it was time to eat. The guests said that they were leaving because they did not want to impose.

"Please stay," John said. "It's better to be with friends than sit around feeling sorry for yourself."

They agreed to stay.

Karen, Terri, and Cynthia prepared the food.

John yelled upstairs to the boys that it was time to eat. They came down in a somber mood.

As the group was eating, Joe attempted to cheer up the boys.

"Boys, your Dad is bringing you to the ranch this weekend," Joe said. "You'll have more fun than you can handle."

"What will we do?" Randy asked.

"We'll ride horses and tour the ranch to see wild animals."

"What kind of animal is there?" Eric asked.

"We have deer, turkey, and wild hogs."

"Can we shoot a deer?" Eric asked.

"No, the season is not open on deer and turkey. However, there's no season on hogs. If we see a young one, we'll shoot it and smoke it for dinner."

The conversation cheered up the boys.

Everybody ate more than they should have eaten and the ladies were kind enough to clean up and wash the dishes. Terri and Karen left. Shortly thereafter, Joe informed John that they must also leave.

"Stay here," John said. "I have two extra bedrooms."

"No, we've already checked into the Anatole. You need private time with your boys."

"Drop in tomorrow."

"We will."

They left.

Eric approached John.

"Dad, Randy and I have been talking. We don't want to go to the funeral."

"Why?"

"Because it'll be too sad."

"You don't need to go if you don't want to. But keep in mind that the purpose is to pay last respects. It's only as sad as you make it. Talk to Randy and let me know what you decide."

"Thanks Dad."

The next morning, the boys told John that they were going to the funeral.

"That's a wise decision," John said. "I'll be next to you if you need me."

"We know you will, Dad," Randy said.

"Saddle up," John said. "We're going to the airport to pick up Grandma, Grandpa, Aunt Cindy, and Uncle Tim. We'll take the Suburban because it has plenty of room."

On the way to John's home, the family began crying. The boys joined the crying. John wanted to cry also but realized he must drive. They arrived at the house and John showed them their accommodations. Shortly thereafter, Joe and Cynthia arrived. They visited for a short period. The mood was somber. Joe realized they needed time together. He and Cynthia left.

The funeral went smoothly. The boys took it much better than John expected. He was proud of them.

Early the next morning, John took the family to the airport. When he returned, he informed the boys that they were leaving for the ranch.

"Do you guys want to take the Suburban or the pickup," John asked. They both wanted to take the pickup truck.

"OK, get you're stuff together and load it in the pickup."

They left at noon and arrived at the ranch at four thirty.

"Do you want to stay in the ranch managers house or here?" Clint asked."

"I want to stay in this big house," Randy replied. "It's way cool."

Clint laughed and said, "That settles it. I'll put you on the second floor. You'll have it all to yourself."

"Thanks Clint," John said.

"No problem. In this remote area of Texas, I enjoy visitors," Clint replied. "You're welcome anytime. I've arranged for a cookout for dinner. We'll eat at six."

John and the boys went upstairs and unpacked. At six, they went down to eat. As usual, Clint had prepared a feast. The boys ate until they were stuffed. Joe informed them that breakfast was at 5:30 and then they would tour the ranch and look for animals.

"John, are they comfortable with a .270," Joe asked. "Or should I take a .257?"

"They can handle a .270," John replied. "They've both shot deer with one and shoot it regularly at the gun club."

"Good. A .257 is a little light for hogs."

After breakfast the next morning, Joe loaded John and his sons into a crew cab pickup and started across the ranch. They were only a short distance from the house when Randy had a question.

"Where are all the animals?" Randy asked.

"They're sneaky," Joe replied. "They hide. You must look for them. Keep you're eyes peeled."

Fifteen minutes later, Eric spotted a herd of deer. Joe stopped the truck and they all watched the deer. After a few minutes, the deer saw them and retreated. Ten minutes later, Joe saw a young hog about seventy yards away. He stopped the truck.

"Do you want to shoot him Randy?" Joe asked.

"No, I don't think I can hit him from here," Randy said.

"I can," Eric said.

"Then get the rifle and do it," Joe responded.

The pig was getting nervous. Eric exited the truck on the opposite side from the animal and bent over so he could not be seen. He went to the back of the truck and rested the rifle on the side of the bed. The pig trotted off to the left. Eric held the crosshairs just behind the shoulder and shot. The pig went down. John jumped out of the truck.

"Son, that was a super shot," John said.

Eric had a big smile on his face.

"Thanks Dad."

Joe retrieved a knife and told him that he would gut the pig. John told Joe that he would help. Joe got a shotgun and told John that it was an anti snake device. Joe informed the boys to stay on the road if they wanted to take a walk. He then told them that if they went into the brush, they were likely to be bitten by a rattlesnake.

John and Joe went to the pig. John volunteered to gut it. While John was working, Joe saw a rattlesnake under a bush about twenty feet away. He shot the snake and cut the rattles off. Joe told John that he was going after another rattle. In a few minutes, John heard him shoot. They dragged the pig back to the truck.

"Eric and Randy," Joe said. "I have something for you to show off to your friends at school."

He pulled a rattle out of his pocket and shook it to show them how it sounded. He gave one to each of them. They rattled them all the way to the ranch.

When they arrived at the ranch, they rode horses. The boys were enjoying it all. In the evening, they dined on the smoked pig. Eric was all smiles because he had provided the meat.

Clint walked over to Eric.

"I heard you made a great shot on that pig," Clint said.

Eric smiled and said, "Thank you sir."

"I want you, your brother, and your Dad to come for a deer hunt when the season opens. Is that OK with you?"

"Wow, that's super."

"Fine. I'll call your Dad to make arrangements when the season is near."

Eric is excited and ran to John to tell him about the invitation.

"Can we come?" Eric asked.

"Sure we can," John replied.

After breakfast the next morning, John thanked everybody for his or her hospitality and left for Dallas.

CHAPTER 14

John returned to the office on Monday. He called in Nick Moore.

"Nick, how did it go?" John asked.

"It went smoothly. I had no problems," Nick replied.

"Were there any complaints?"

"None."

"Good. Thanks for helping me out."

"You're welcome. Actually, I enjoyed it."

"I intend to add several new brokers. I'll need an assistant manager. Are you interested?"

"Can I work my book?"

"Yes."

"Count me in."

"Great. I need to touch base with Kent and we'll discuss it sometime this week. You can get back to your business."

Nick left.

Terri came into John's office.

"John, are you doing OK?" Terri asked.

"Yeah, I'm making it," John answered.

"If there is anything I can do, please let me know."

"I appreciate that. And by the way, the turkey dinner was delicious."

"Thanks. Keep in mind that there are very few women, these days, that can cook."

John smiled and said, "That talent is etched in my mind."

"I need to get back to my brokers."

"I'll talk to you later."

John got a call from Don Logan.

"One of your brokers is trying to rip me off," Don said.

"Who?" John asked.

"Jim."

Jim was the short-term stock trader.

"In what way?" John asked.

"My only investment with him is a hundred shares of BMR. I've had it for a long time and have made good money on it. He called me today and said they are rapidly losing market share and are experiencing financial difficulties. That's a bunch of bullshit. Apparently, he's not satisfied with the commissions he's making from me," Don said.

"I'll call up the news on the stock."

John operated his CRT and found that Jim's story was correct.

"Don, he's telling you the truth. I would make the same recommendation," John said.

"I'm not selling," Don stated.

"That's your privilege."

Don hung up. John called in Jim.

"Jim, I want to let you know that Don Logan called and said you were trying to rip him off," John said.

Jim was furious.

"What the hell is going on? All I did was tell him what was going on with BMR and advised him to get into a better stock," Jim said.

"Calm down. Apparently he's in love with the stock. I verified the information you gave him and told him I would have done the same thing. You know what I would do?"

"What?"

"I would have the stock certificate mailed to him and close the account."

"I'll do it immediately. Thanks for your help."

"Jim, when you're honest, I'll support you one hundred percent."

"I know you will."

Jim returned to his desk and called Don Logan.

"Don, this is Jim. I'm informing you that I'm mailing your stock certificate to you and closing your account."

"You can't do that," Don said.

"Yes, I can. It's obvious that you don't trust me as your broker. It's in both of our best interests to terminate the relationship. You can easily find another broker at a different firm."

"I'm calling the SEC."

"That's your prerogative."

Don hung up.

Jim went to John's office.

"I did what you suggested and he said he's calling the SEC," Jim said.

"Don't worry about it, I'll take care of it," John said.

"Can I get a complaint from this?"

"No way. I told you that I would handle it."

"Thanks John."

Jim left.

Kenny Sampson walked into John's office.

"John, I screwed up," Kenny said.

"How?" John asked.

"I put the wrong symbol on a trade slip and the stock is heading south."

"I'll take care of it but you'll eat the loss."

"I know. I just want to stop the bleeding."

John picked up the phone, called Damon's traders on the floor of the exchange, and sold the stock.

"Kenny, you got twenty and a half for it," John said.

"Damn, that's a thousand dollar hickey," Kenny said.

"It was an expensive lesson."

"You're right about that."

Kenny went back to work. John called Kent.

"Kent, John. I have eight empty desks. When are you going to send me some trainees?"

"You have three coming next week and three the following week," Kent said.

"That's great. By the way, I feel that I need an assistant manager. I believe that Nick Moore is an excellent candidate. What do you think?"

"You're right. Your branch is one of the few without an assistant. Do it."

John hung up and called in Nick.

"Do you still want to be the assistant manager?" John asked.

"If the deal is right," Nick replied.

"You can keep your book and receive an additional thirty thousand a year. Will that work?"

"That dog will hunt."

"OK, you're the assistant manager as of now."

John called a meeting.

"The branch is growing and will continue to grow," John said. "We'll have six trainees in the next two weeks. As result, we need an assistant manager. That person is Nick. Do you have anything to say, Nick?"

"Yes, I will adhere to the same philosophy that John has. Be honest with your clients. I'm here to support you if you follow that guideline," Nick said.

John told them that the branch needed more brokers. He informed them if they had a friend that was a good producer, to have them call him. He then said that if they were hired, dinner for two was on him.

The following Monday, the three trainees arrived. John met with them.

"Your main mission at this point is to pass the Series Seven test," John said. "If you're having trouble, let me know and I'll get you help. Unfortunately, the firm's policy is that you get only one try to pass it. If you adhere to the study program, you shouldn't have a problem passing. Are there any questions?"

"How does the study program work?" a trainee asked.

"You do one lesson a day, take a test on what you covered, and give your score to my secretary, Karen. Then review the study guide to determine the answers to the questions you missed. Instructions are in the guide."

John passed out study guides and escorted them to their work place. Melissa entered John's office.

"I have a client problem that I don't know how to handle," she said.

"Tell me about it," John said.

"I have this guy in mutual funds. He's not satisfied with his return. He says that his friends at other firms are doubling their money every six months."

"He's full of that stuff that cows drop."

"I know."

"Is he in the firms funds and if so, how long has he held them?"

"About three years."

"Then he still has a small commission to get out of them. Tell him to contact one of the brokers that double money every six months and you will waive the outgoing commission."

"That sounds great. I'll do it."

Melissa called the client.

"Carlos, this is Melissa. I have a solution to your problem concerning return on your investment."

"Super. What is it?" Carlos asked.

"I'll waive the commission to liquidate your funds. That will enable you to hire one of the brokers that are doubling money every six months."

"I don't know if I want to do that."

"Why?"

"Maybe I embellished the returns. I was trying to find out if you had something better. I want you to be my broker."

"I'll do it if you promise not to pull any more tricks on me."

"It's a deal."

"I'll be in contact."

They hung up.

The next day, John received a call from a broker with another firm.

"John, this is Larry Johnson. A friend at your firm said you were looking for brokers. Can we get together?"

"Sure. When can you come?" John asked.

"After the market closes today."

"I'll see you then."

Larry showed up at four o'clock. He was escorted to John's office. The two introduced themselves.

"I'm happy that you are interested in Damon," John said. "How long have you been in the business?"

"Ten years," Larry replied.

"That means you're a survivor. Why do you want to leave your present firm?"

"Because I don't get along with the manager."

"I've been there. That's a valid reason."

"Yeah, no purpose is served by being miserable."

"Larry, what's your production?"

"About three hundred thousand a year."

Larry opened his brief case and gives John documentation.

"How much of it can you bring with you?" John asked.

"At least three fourths and probably more," Larry answered.

"How many complaints have you had?"

"Only one in ten years."

"That's a good record. What would it take to get you over here?"

"I believe that a fifty thousand signing bonus is fair."

"Are you prepared to make a decision today?"

"Yes."

"If you'll give me a couple minutes of privacy, we may be able to close this deal."

"OK, I'll tour the branch."

John called Kent and related the details. Kent said that Larry was in the ballpark on the bonus and to do the deal. John instructed Karen to find Larry and bring him to his office. Larry walked in.

"Larry, welcome to the team. It's a done deal. However, the offer is contingent upon verification of your complaint record."

"That will not be a problem."

"When can you start?"

"I'll need three or four days to set my clients up to transfer their accounts."

"Call me when you have it done."

CHAPTER 15

John had become attracted to Terri. He called her to his office.

"Terri, I'm feeling hungry. Would you like to go to dinner tonight?" John asked.

"That sounds great. I thought you would never ask," Terri said.

"I'll pick you up at seven. Where do you live?"

Terri told him and gave him directions to her apartment.

"Do you like steak?" John asked.

"What Texan doesn't?"

"Then we'll go to Bob's Steak House."

"That's super."

"I'll see you at seven. By the way, don't dress sexy because you may excite me."

Terri laughed and said, "I'll try not to do that."

John picked up Terri at seven. They drove to the restaurant.

"John, I really appreciate this invitation. I've wanted to go out with you for a long time," Terri said.

"Thanks. I've had my eye on you also," John said.

They arrived at the restaurant. The waiter came over and they ordered. John also ordered a bottle of good wine.

"John, how do like being the manager?" Terri asked.

"It's OK. There's good and bad, but the good out weighs the bad," John replied.

"What's the bad?"

"Dealing with personnel problems and sometimes firing people."

"I can understand that. What's the good?"

"Many of the brokers have cleaned up their acts and are being honest with their clients. I've had to fire much fewer than I expected."

"Almost everyone thinks that you're a good manager. The brokers say that you're fair and you will go to bat for them if they follow the rules."

"That's good to hear."

"Has anyone ever accused you of being idealistic?"

"Yes, but that's the way I lead my life. I can be pragmatic when I need to. However, I'll never bend on my principles."

"That's commendable."

"What's going on in your life?"

"Nothing exciting. I take my little trips to the malls and occasionally go to a movie. I also enjoy riding horses at my parent's place. I also do volunteer work."

"What kind of volunteer work do you do?"

"I work at a crisis center and take calls from people in distress. Some of them are suicidal."

"That sounds depressing."

"Not really. If you help one person, you've accomplished something."

"Don't call me idealistic again. You're more idealistic than I. I compliment you for caring."

"Thanks John."

They finished the meal and ordered dessert.

"Would you like to see me again?" John asked.

"I would love to," Terri answered.

"I must tell you that a lot of our dates will be at my house because I don't want the boys to feel deserted. Is that acceptable?"

"That's not a problem."

"Tomorrow night, I'm cooking burgers for Randy's baseball team. I need another supervisor. Are you up to that?"

"That sounds like fun. I'll do it."

"You're a brave woman. I'm taking off tomorrow to handle the logistics.

After work, come to the house. Bring something casual and you can change there. I promise not to look."

"What if I want you to look?"

John laughed and said, "I'm not sure I could handle it. Also, fifteen kids present complicate the situation even further."

"I'll defer to your judgment."

"Terri, your logic amazes me."

"I can become illogical at times."

"Can't we all?"

John took Terri to her apartment. They kissed goodnight and John left. On the way home, John thought to himself that Terri was a special person.

After work the following day, Terri went to John's house and took her casual clothes.

"Where do I change?" she asked John.

"In any of the bedrooms or bathrooms," John replied.

"Do you mind telling me where they are?"

"You're so demanding."

"Give me a break."

John took her on a tour of the house. She then mingled with the team. She joked with Randy. He asked her to play a computer game. She agreed. After the game, he returned to his friends.

The burgers were finally ready. The team ate outside and Terri and John ate in the dining room. Randy joined them.

"Dad, is she going to be our new mother," Randy asked.

"John smiles and says, "We're only friends at this point."

"She would make a good mother."

"Why?"

"Because she's pretty and fun."

"You're very perceptive."

"Terri, would you be our mother?" Randy asked.

"Randy, your father and I haven't discussed it. If we do, I'm sure that you'll be the first to know."

Randy picked up his plate and joined the team.

"I have one vote," Terri said.

"Yeah, but my vote is the only one that counts," John stated.

"You are so bad. You don't even believe in democracy."

John chuckled and told Terri that they needed to check on the team. He then told her that any woman that can impress his son deserved a hug and kiss. They embraced and exchanged a long kiss.

The next day, John returned to the branch. Soon after he arrived, Nick entered his office.

"John, we have a problem," Nick said.

"What is it?"

"Gus is taking payments from clients."

"How do you know?"

"When he went to lunch yesterday, two of the brokers noticed two checks on his desk and informed me. I got the names from the checks and called the clients."

"What did they say?"

"They told me that Gus said that he was a certified financial planner and could guarantee them a twenty percent return. He also told them that it was a fee-based proposition. He related to them that the fee would maintain his objectivity and he wouldn't consider commissions."

"What a snake. The only thing he's certified in is lying. Get his ass in here."

Nick brought Gus to John's office.

"What's going on John?" Gus asked.

"You've been taking money from your clients," John answered.

"That's not true."

"We have proof."

"I know what the problem is. I've loaned money to a few of my clients and they're paying me back."

"That's not what they say."

"So what's wrong with making a little extra money on the side?"

"Because it's against NASD rules and is unethical. Furthermore, it's immoral because you lied to them to get the money. This offence results in automatic license revocation."

"Surely you'll not report this."

"Yes I will."

"I'll pay you not to."

"I'm not on the take. Nick will escort you to your desk to get your personal effects. I want you out of the office within ten minutes."

Nick escorted Gus to his desk. Gus put his book in his briefcase. Nick told him that he could not do that.

"It's my damn property," Gus said.

"No it's not. Give it to me," Nick stated.

Gus became angry. He made a fist and hit Nick in the face. Nick retaliated by hitting Gus so hard that he fell to the floor. Gus was semi conscience. Meanwhile, Nick retrieved the book. When Gus was able to function, Nick escorted him to the elevator and told him that his personal effects would be sent to him via UPS.

Nick walked into John's office with a bleeding nose.

"What the hell happened?" John asked.

Nick told him.

"Do you want to file assault charges?" John asked.

"No, I got the best of him. He'll not forget it," Nick said.

"From this day forward, you're the official enforcer in this branch."

"Thanks a lot."

"Do you need to go home and change shirts?"

"No, I'll show off my battle scars."

"I see. You're a real macho man. I'll call you Rocky."

"Think of something better. I can beat Rocky."

They both laughed. Nick left.

John called Kent and explained the events to him.

"Kent, I'm calling a meeting to pass out his accounts. I propose to tell the brokers to contact the clients immediately and ask them if they paid him. If so, the firm will reimburse them."

"You're right on. We're obligated."

"Thanks Kent. I'll talk to you later."

John called the meeting, related the details, and told them what to do. He then passed out the accounts. He called Nick to the front and pointed to the blood on his shirt.

"I've renamed him Rocky," John said.

This brought a roar of laughter from the brokers. Nick said that he wanted to make a statement.

"Now you know that I have a vicious right fist," Nick said. "If you want to enter into combat with me, I prefer that you warn me. That will enable me to take the first punch."

The brokers laughed again. One of the female brokers rushed to the front. She kissed Nick on the cheek and announced that Rocky was her hero.

"Rocky, do you intend to take all the women?" one of the male brokers asked.

"Yes, I'll take them all. You guys will need to search elsewhere," Nick said.

John ended the fun by adjourning the meeting.

CHAPTER 16

Larry, the broker from another firm, walked into John's office.

"Larry, I thought you needed a few days," John said." What happened?"

"Someone overheard a conversation with a client and reported me. They fired me. I have my client list. All I need is a phone," Larry replied.

John laughed and said, "Everybody gets fired at least once. I'll show you to your desk."

Larry worked hard on transferring accounts. By the end of the month, he was near the top in production. John took him to lunch.

"Larry, you're doing a good job," John said. "How do you like it here?"

"It's great. The atmosphere is positive here and the brokers are friendly," Larry answered.

"I'm glad you like it. I have only two rules. First, be honest with your clients. Secondly, work hard to keep your production up."

"Those are also my rules."

"What are your aspirations?"

"I don't want the hassle of being a manager. I want to be a top producer and provide a good living for my family."

"That's an honorable goal. Do you have children?"

"Yes, two sons."

"That's what I have. Sooner or later, we'll be accused of discrimination."

They both laughed. John paid the tab and they returned to the branch.

Shortly after John arrived, he decided to leave his office and check on the day's production. When he was almost to the door, Gus, the fired broker, walked in and pulled out a 9mm semiautomatic pistol.

"I'm going to kill you," Gus said.

"Why?" John asked.

"Because you ruined my life."

"Gus, I did what I had to do. Can we talk about this?"

"No."

John realized that Gus was serious. John quickly sidestepped and placed his index finger between the hammer and firing pin of the pistol and gripped the weapon. He then kneed Gus in the groin. Gus loosened his grip on the gun and John took it from him. He told Gus to get face down on the floor with his hands straight out and placed his foot over a kidney. In the meantime, one of the brokers called 911. Gus was slowly moving his right hand towards his pants pocket. John noticed an outline of a pistol in the pocket. He stomped on Gus' kidney. Gus grimaced with pain. John retrieved the pistol.

"You just made a big mistake," John said.

"What?" Gus asked.

"By pulling that stupid move, you'll piss blood for a week."

"If you'll let me go, I promise not to threaten you again."

"No way. You've shown your colors."

The police arrived, took a statement from John, and left with Gus in handcuffs.

Nick entered John's office.

"The brokers have given you a new name," Nick said.

"I anticipated some repercussions. What's the name?" John asked.

"Rambo."

"That's an insult. I can handle Rambo any day. Why didn't they name me superman?"

"I don't know, but I think Rambo will stick."

"Tell the troops that there will be free beer at five. Get a head count of those coming."

At four o'clock, John sent two brokers to purchase the beer. When they returned, they asked John where to put it. John took them to the meeting room. He noticed that one of the containers was open.

"Why is this open?" John asked.

"We felt that it was our duty to sample the beer to make sure it wasn't poisoned. We would never forgive ourselves if the entire office was deceased," one of the brokers said.

"You are honorable men. Give me my change."

"What about the tip?"

"There isn't one."

They gave him the change.

The party started at five. Everybody was having a good time. Nick called them all to attention.

"I propose a toast to Rambo, our fearless leader," Nick said.

They all laughed and toasted.

Terri was staying close to John.

One of the brokers walked up to them.

"There is a rumor that you two are dating. Is that a true story?" he asked.

"That's a true story," John replied.

"How can an ugly guy like you latch on to Terri? I've been pursuing her for months."

"Apparently, I have something you don't have."

"What is it?"

"That's proprietary information."

"Please tell me the secret formula. I can use it on other women."

"No, you couldn't handle the overwhelming attention."

Terri kissed the broker on the cheek.

"That's your consolation prize," she said.

Everybody laughed.

"John, you're the best manager I've had. You've cleaned up the branch. And unlike the previous manager, you seem to care about the brokers," the broker said.

"I appreciate that," John said.

The beer was almost gone. However, Nick was not finished with his fun. He had the brokers chant Rambo repeatedly. Then everyone left. John told Terri that he needed to relieve the sitter and asked her if she wanted to come over for grilled steaks. She agreed. They met at John's house.

When John arrived, he paid the sitter and asked her where the boys were. She said that they were upstairs playing on their computers. He shouted for them to come down because Terri was coming.

When Terri arrived, both of the boys hugged her. John went outside to start the fire.

"Why don't you marry my Dad," Randy asked.

"Because he hasn't asked me," Terri replied.

"I'll tell him to. I want you to be my next Mother."

"Thanks for the help."

"I also want you to join the family," Eric said.

"I appreciate the support you guys have given me," Terri said.

"If he asked you, would you accept?"

"In a heart beat."

John came in.

"Dad, we have something important to discuss," Eric said.

"What's that?" John asked.

"We want Terri to be a family member. She said that she would accept a proposal if you asked."

John smiled.

"Terri, I see that you've been working behind the scenes," John said.

"I'm not the one who brought it up," she replied.

"With this kind of pressure on me, I have no choice," John said.

John kneels on one knee.

"Terri, will you be my wife?"

"I would love to."

They hugged and kissed. The boys clapped and cheered.

John iced down a bottle of champagne to celebrate. They sipped on the champagne. The boys had soft drinks. It was late when the champagne was finished. Terri said she needed to get some sleep. John escorted her to the door and kissed her goodnight.

The next morning at the office, John called Joe at the ranch. Joe answered the phone.

"What's going on, rancher?" John asked.

"Hard work. What's happening with you?" Joe asked.

"I need for you to reciprocate."

"On what?"

"Best man."

"You're kidding. Who would marry you?"

"Terri."

"You lucky dog. You must lead a charmed life. She's the best looking woman in Dallas County."

"When you're as handsome as I, you get these breaks."

"In your dreams. John, I'll be honored to be your best man. By the way, if you want to spend your honeymoon at the ranch, you're welcome. You and Terri can stay in the ranch managers house for privacy and we'll put the boys up in the ranch house."

"That sounds good. I'll discuss it with Terri."

Thirty minutes later, Terri called Cynthia, who had been a close friend. Joe answered the phone.

"Joe, Terri. I need to speak with Cynthia," Terri said.

"Congratulations," Joe said.

"How did you know?"

"Mental telepathy. Here comes Cynthia."

"Cynthia, how's the baby?" Terri asked.

"She's great but it's a lot of work," Cynthia answered.

"I want you to be my bridesmaid."

"I would love to. When's the wedding?"

"We don't know yet. I'll let you know. I need to get back to work. I'll call you tonight."

The day was uneventful for John. He asked Terri to dinner and made arrangements for a sitter.

They arrived at the restaurant and ordered.

"Terri, are you certain that you want to marry a man who is ten years your senior and has two kids?" John asked.

"I've never been more certain of anything in my life," Terri said.

"Then it's a done deal. Do you want a large wedding or a simple one?"

"I'm a country girl. I prefer things simple."

"OK, I believe that it is customary for the bride to make the arrangements."

Terri smiled and said, "You male chauvinist pig."

John laughed.

"There may be some credence to that. However, if I mess it up, it could ruin our marriage. Which do you prefer?" John asked.

"I'm forced to do it," Terri replied.

"You're a good woman. Where do you want to go on the honeymoon?"

"To the planet Krypton."

"That's too expensive. Where else?"

"John, I really don't care. In fact, I don't care if we take a honeymoon. As long as I'm with you, I'll be happy."

"There are a couple of possibilities. Joe invited us to the ranch. We can also go to northwest Arkansas. It's beautiful. There are many rivers, streams, and lakes in the hills. The boys love it. We'll be in facilities most of time but we'll need to camp out some. What do you think?"

"Let's go for it. There is one caveat. Will we be sharing rooms and tents with the boys?"

"I like that question. You sound like you want to get passionate. There will be no sharing of rooms or tents."

CHAPTER 17

John circulated among the brokers and informed them there would be a meeting with Gary Robinson, the limited partnership representative, after the market closed.

John returned to his office. Tim, one of the brokers from the last training class, was waiting. He wanted to tell John that he had dropped a very large ticket. John congratulated him.

"Where did you get the lead?" John asked.

"It was a referral," Tim replied.

"What does that tell you?"

"There's money to be made from them. However, I don't know how to ask for referrals. This one came out of the blue."

"First of all, you ask the client if they're happy with you. If they say yes, tell them that you are trying to increase your business. Ask them if they know someone that can use your services. Obviously, if they say they're not happy, forget it."

"That makes sense. I'll do it."

"Keep up the good work."

"I'll do my best."

"That's all that anybody can expect."

Thirty minutes before the market closed, Gary Robinson walked into John's office.

"How's it going?" Gary asked.

"Great. Branch profits are up and we're getting almost no complaints. How is it with you?" John asked.

"Not well. I'm still trying to overcome the last fiasco. John, I need your help."

"How?"

"I want you to pressure your brokers to put their clients in the partnerships."

"I can't do that. They know what's suitable for their clients. I don't."

"If you'll do it for me, I'll put in a good word to the big boys in New York. That may get you a promotion."

"And if I don't?"

"Then I'll be forced to tell them that you don't have the firms best interests in mind."

"Gary, get the hell out of my office. Now."

Gary left. John considered canceling the meeting. He decided that would only add fuel to the fire and allowed it to proceed.

The brokers went to the meeting room. Gary greeted them and told them that the failures of the past were an aberration. He stated that the people responsible had been fired and replaced by some of the best experts in the country.

"I want to tell you about an exciting investment," Gary said. "We are introducing a partnership that invests in commodities. The manager has an excellent track record. We're projecting a forty percent return. In addition, the commission is ten percent. How does that sound?"

"Is this the manager that managed the windmill project?" a broker asked.

This brought a laugh.

"No, we fired him."

"We were taught that commodities are risky," another broker said.

"Sure, but a lot of investors will take some risk for a forty percent return. Do you have any more questions?"

"Do you have anything better?" a broker asked.

"If your clients are conservative, I have the perfect investment. We have a partnership that buys medium size companies that are either at breakeven or have a slight loss. We'll turn them around and the value of the company will increase tremendously."

"How will you turn them around?" a broker asked.

"We'll hire proven turn around artists and put them in charge of the companies."

"Why didn't you hire these guys to turn around the last wave of partnerships that went belly up?" a broker asked.

The room vibrated with laughter. Gary hesitated.

"That was a different situation. As I said, we have taken care of that problem," Gary said. "Many fortunes have been made using these same tactics."

"How many fortunes have been lost?" a broker asked.

"You have a negative attitude. You'll never make it in this business."

"You may be right. I'm the number two broker in the branch. I'll probably never be number one. Why are you trying to increase commissions at the client's expense? Also, why are you trying to make the broker suffer by losing clients? I'll not invest a dime in any of your partnerships."

Again, the brokers had a good laugh. Gary was livid. He motioned for John to come outside the room.

"John, I'll have your job for this. You set me up," Gary said.

"You're paranoid. I haven't mentioned the meeting to the brokers," John stated.

"Yeah, right."

Gary left the office in anger. John entered the meeting room.

"Gary surrendered. He made a strategic retreat. The meeting is over," John said.

The brokers applauded and left.

The next morning, John received a call from Kent.

"How's it going?" Kent asked.

"It's going well," John replied.

"I got a call from my boss in New York. He said that Gary said that you were uncooperative, didn't care about the firm, and set him up for a negative response from the brokers."

John related what transpired.

"What an asshole. I'll take care of it. His track record is not exactly stellar."

That afternoon, John got a call from Gary.

"John, I'm up to my ass in alligators. I need your help," Gary said.

"What kind of help?" John asked.

"I need for you to tell the truth about setting me up. I'll make sure that it's swept under the rug and you'll not suffer from it."

"I can't recant something that I told the truth about."

"John, my job is at stake."

"All of our jobs are at stake every day."

"How much money would it take to convince you to say you set me up?"

"One hundred million."

"Let's get serious about this."

"Gary, I don't need your damn money. Goodbye."

Within a week, Gary's employment was terminated. Soon thereafter, Claude, the number two broker, entered John's office.

"John, I'm worried," Claude said.

"About what?" John asked.

"I put down Gary. He'll probably talk to the big boys and get me fired."

"What do I preach to the brokers?"

"To be honest."

"And you were. If you're honest, you'll never suffer as long as Nick or me manage this branch. You were honest."

"That statement relieves a burden."

"There's another factor at work here."

"What's that?"

"Gary is no longer with the firm."

"I hate to see anyone fall upon bad times, but he was a discredit to the firm."

"You're right. I appreciate the effort you have put out for the branch. Now, get your butt out there and shoot for number one."

Claude smiled and left.

John got a call from Kent. He wanted to meet John over a beer when the market closed. John agreed. They met at The Point in Addison and ordered beer.

"John, I may be in trouble," Kent said.

"Over what?" John asked.

"The boys in New York don't think the region is generating enough commissions."

"Hell, I've got record profits and from what I hear, most of the other branches do too."

"Yeah, but you're way ahead of the pack. They want the other's to match your performance."

"That's ridiculous."

"Maybe so, but that's the way the wind is blowing. I want you to know that if I go, you'll still have a job."

"No, I'll not, because if you go, I go."

"I appreciate the support, but don't be stupid."

"I'm not. I don't need this job."

"There's another thing in the works that concerns me. They want to cut broker's commissions and link the percentage to the amount of production."

"That encourages brokers to do anything for production."

"You're right."

"We'll probably lose some good brokers."

"I doubt it. Apparently all the firms have gotten together and will do the same thing."

"Doesn't this industry care about the client?"

"I wonder. I think they look upon them as cash cows."

"That sucks."

"Yes, it does. Thanks for giving me an ear that listens. By the way, when's the wedding?"

"Saturday afternoon."

"Are you sure you can handle a young wife?"

"No, but I'll have fun trying."

They both laughed and then left.

CHAPTER 18

The day of the wedding finally arrived. Joe and Cynthia showed up on Saturday morning with two bottles of champagne iced down.

"It's too damn early to drink," John said.

"No it's not," Joe replied. "Anything goes on a wedding day."

They uncorked the champagne and began to drink it.

"Terri, why didn't you wait on me?" Joe asked.

"Because Cynthia would have killed both of us," Terri replied.

"Terri, you wouldn't want him," Cynthia said. "All he wants to do is round up cattle and shoot wild animals and birds."

"How's the daughter?" Terri asked Cynthia.

"She's a joy. Joe loves her, but he wants a boy so that he'll have someone to hunt with."

"Yeah, and I have a formula to ensure that a boy is propagated," Joe said.

"What's that?" John asked.

"I can't reveal it. If I do, there will be a preponderance of males and few females. That means that the species will be endangered."

That drew a laugh. Terri and Cynthia were getting a little tipsy and decided to take a nap. Joe and John consumed time by talking about the ranch and the office. When the ladies awoke, they all went out for lunch. Joe and Cynthia wanted to shop tomorrow before returning to the ranch. John gave them a key to the house.

That afternoon, they proceeded to the church for the wedding. They were married and John kissed the bride. The kiss was rather long and passionate. This encouraged everybody to chuckle.

After the reception, the newlyweds proceeded to their house. The Suburban was loaded and ready for the trip to Arkansas. They ordered pizza and began the trip.

Just at dark, they arrived in Hot Springs National Park. They rented two hotel rooms and went to McClard's Barbecue for dinner. They all stuff themselves on the one of a kind treat. The next day, they took in the tourist attractions and went to the observation tower on the mountain. Next, they toured Lake Ouachita, one of the very few lakes in the country with zero pollution. The lake is surrounded by forest. Terri said that she would like to live on this lake. John told her that was not possible because no houses were allowed on the lake. He explained that this policy was a major reason there was no pollution. They returned to town and drank the mineral water from the springs. They liked it. They purchased several plastic containers and filled them with the mineral water. The water was free.

Early the next morning, they headed north.

"Dad, where are we going?" Randy asked.

"To Mountain View," John replied.

"What's there?"

"Mountains, beautiful scenery, and the White River. We'll go Rainbow trout fishing on the White."

"Are bears up there?" Eric asked.

"Yes, but our odds of seeing one are slim," John replied.

Everybody enjoyed the scenery on the way there. They arrived at ten A.M. John decided to camp on a creek he liked. John and the boys pitched two tents. John gave Eric a 9MM pistol. He left the boys with Terri and went to the lone food store in town to purchase food. While in town, he acquired a stout cane pole, a frog gig, and a cotter pin.

Everyone had lunch and they went to Jack's Landing to hire a guide for trout fishing. The guide's name was Bubba Smith. He was about 5'11", weighed approximately two hundred sixty pounds, and had a belly to rival that of a Sumo wrestler. He told them that he went by the name of Big Bubba. They loaded into a large Jon boat and journeyed up river for forty-five minuets.

Big Bubba stopped the outboard engine.

"I got me some live worms and some whole kernel corn," Big Bubba said. "We'll bait the hooks half and half. That way, we'll find out what these here fishes are bitin'. This here deep hole we're comin' up on has a ton of trout; so get your lines out."

They all caught a trout from the hole. The boys and Terri were excited. Big Bubba fired up the engine and went upstream from the hole. This pass, only Eric and Terri caught a fish. They tried the hole one more time and only John scored.

"There's not as many fishes in this hole as I thunk," Big Bubba said. "We'll drift the shallows. That's probably where they're hidin'."

They drifted the shallows and caught fish on a regular basis. By the middle of the afternoon, they all had their limit of six. The boat returned to the dock. They unloaded and returned to camp.

John fried the trout, complete with French fries and hush puppies. Everybody feasted on the trout.

John then retrieved the cane pole, the gig, and cotter pin. He then lit the Coleman stove. A coat hanger was heated until it was red. The cane pole was cut off at a strong point. The gig was positioned on the pole and the coat hanger was used to burn two holes in the pole. The cotter pin was placed through the holes and the ends of the pin were bent back to secure the gig to the pole. A frog gig now existed.

At dark, John issued battery-powered headlamps to everyone and they waded the creek in search of bullfrogs. Terri was a little leery of this venture, but goes along for the ride. John showed the boys how to gig a frog and then turned this duty over to them.

"Guys, there's a lot of cottonmouths in this creek," John said. "You know what they look like; so keep your eyes alert "

"What's a cottonmouth?" Terri asked.

"It's a poisonous snake," John replied.

"Oh no. What have I gotten myself into?"

John laughs and said, "Don't worry about it. Stay close to me and you'll survive without a snake bite."

"How can you be so confident?"

"Because I know nature and snakes."

"I think you're jaded."

"Perhaps, but I've only been bitten once."

"Great record. Why are you still alive?"

"Because less than one percent of the people bitten die. Those that do are usually children or people with medical problems."

They gigged ten large bullfrogs and returned to camp. John showed the boys how to clean the frogs and turned it over to them.

"I want to go trout fishing again tomorrow," Randy said.

"Yeah, that was fun," Eric added.

"I'll need to check with your new mother," John said.

He summoned Terri.

"Are you up to another fishing trip?" John asked.

"Sure thing. It was fun," Terri replied.

They retired to the tents.

The next morning, they arose before first light. John fired up the Coleman stove and cooked frog legs, eggs, and fried biscuits. Everyone enjoyed this delicacy. They then headed for the boat dock.

John requested Big Bubba and was told that he had another party. John asked if there could be a guide switch. The owner said that he would check on it and walked off.

Big Bubba sauntered over to them.

"OK, let's go catch us some fishes," he said.

They went to the same hole and caught a few trout. Then they drifted with the current. While they were drifting, John struck up a conversation with Big Bubba.

"Do you guide for a living?" John asked.

"Naw, I have a farm, but I ain't makin' much money off it. I do this to fatten my wallet," Bubba answered.

"Do you have children?"

"You bet. I got me four of them. Three boys and one girl. I'm tryin' ever night to get me some more."

He roared with laughter at his last comment.

"Why don't you give your wife a break?" Terri asked.

"Hey, she was born and bred to do what she's doin'. She likes it. Anyways, if you keep them barefoot and pregnant, you don't have no problems," Bubba replied.

Terri quit the conversation in disgust.

They again caught their limit of trout and returned to the dock and then to the campsite. They spent the afternoon exploring the forest. Deer, squirrels, and rabbits were observed. Eric was disappointed because no bears were present. John gathered some edible wild mushrooms to compliment dinner.

The next morning, they broke camp and journeyed north towards Mountain Home. On the way, they stopped frequently to observe interesting sights. They finally arrived and rented two cottages on Lake Norfork. They fished from the bank and caught enough for dinner.

The next morning, they decided to tour the lake. They rented a party barge and John loaded the grill. The sights on and around the lake were observed. John grilled hamburgers and hot dogs for lunch. Terri commented that this part of Arkansas was beautiful country.

The next day, they went to Rogers and drove around Lake Beaverfork. The area was scenic and was a major retirement center. Everyone believed that it was too crowded. They proceeded to Fayetteville, the home of the University of Arkansas. They toured the campus and spent the night in town.

Early the next morning, they set course for Fort Smith. On the way, John informed them that they would tour a museum detailing the deeds of the hanging judge.

"Who was the hanging judge?" Eric asked.

"His name was Judge Parker," John replied. "He was a frontier judge who would hang a man for any misdeed he deemed serious. At the museum, you can see the jail they were kept in before hanging. The gallows were also there. Inside the courtroom, pictures of most of his victims, along with their backgrounds, are on the wall. It's a very interesting place," John said.

When they arrived, the first thing they went to was the jail. It was located below an elevated portion of the courthouse. The floors were dirt.

There were no windows, running water, or heat. The only source of light was the space between the bars of the door. The restroom consisted of wooden buckets. It made Alcatraz look like a mansion. Terri and the boys were awed by its austerity.

They then viewed the gallows.

"Dad, exactly how does hanging kill them?" Eric inquired.

"The knot on the rope is positioned so that, when they release the trap, their neck is snapped just below the brain. That usually does it. If not, they choke to death."

They entered the courtroom. The pictures and backgrounds fascinated everybody. Some of the victims did not do much to get hanged.

The nose of the Suburban is pointed southwest towards Dallas.

"You guys got a history lesson today," Terri said.

"Yeah, I must do a paper for History," Eric said. "I intend to read about this and then relate my personal experience."

"That would be great."

They arrived home. One of the neighbors came by and asked if the boys could come to her daughter's birthday party. The boys were all for it and left.

"Terri, now that you are my lovely wife, there are some things you should know," John said. "My first wife was killed by a delivery truck driven by a drunk driver. I settled two weeks ago for three million. With what I had, my net worth is now close to five million. You and the boys will be taken care of when I kick the bucket. My new will and details of my investments are in my safety deposit box. Eric has access and we'll get you on it next week."

Are you telling me I married a sugar daddy?" Terri asked.

John laughed and said, "I didn't tell you I was a wife beater."

"For that kind of money, I'll take a beating."

They hugged and kissed and walked to the bedroom.

CHAPTER 19

On Monday, John returned to the office. He went through his correspondence and saw a memo from Ben Freid that requested that all branch managers report for a meeting at eight tomorrow morning. He called in his secretary.

"Who the hell is Ben Freid?" he asked.

"The new regional manager," she replied.

"You're kidding."

"Unfortunately, I'm not."

John was upset. He wadded up the memo and threw it against the wall. He then went to Nick's office.

"Nick, what happened to Kent?" John asked.

"They axed him and brought in this jerk from New York," Nick replied.

"Why do you call him a jerk?"

"He was in the branch when you were gone. He called a meeting and told the brokers that production was not high enough and that they should use any means to get it up. You'll not believe his next statement. He said to emphasize the positive about the investment and ignore the negative."

"That sucks. It appears that he believes in the screw the client syndrome."

"I think you're right."

"He's called a meeting for tomorrow morning. I'll let you know what transpires."

John toured the office and talked with the brokers. They all expressed concern about the new regional manager. John returned to his office in disgust. Larry, the top producer, entered John's office.

"John, I can't do what Ben is asking," Larry said.

"Then don't," John replied.

"But I'm afraid I'll get fired if I don't do it."

"Over my dead body. Don't worry about it. Even if you do get fired, you'll be a hot commodity with other firms."

"I guess you're right. Let me know how the meeting goes."

"I will."

The next morning, John went to the meeting.

Ben entered the room and introduced himself. He told them that production was much too low and that if it did not improve dramatically, they would be fired.

"What are your expectations?" a branch manager asked.

"My goal is to double production by the end of the next twelve months." Ben replied. "To achieve this, I demand monthly improvement."

"Do you have any suggestions on how to accomplish this?" another manager asked.

"Yes. Change the way your brokers think. They're salesmen, not financial gurus. When you buy a car, does the salesman tell you the bad points about the car? Hell no. Therefore, tell your brokers to ignore this risk bullshit unless the client asks. If the client is dumb enough to invest unwisely, it's his fault. In other words, tell them what they want to hear. The bottom line is what counts."

"What about the legal implications of that philosophy," a manager asked.

"No guts, no glory," Ben replied.

Numerous hands were raised for questions. Ben looked around and decided that he did not want to field that many questions. He stated that he had an appointment and dismissed the managers.

John walked to Ben and requested a conference. They went to Ben's office.

"Congratulations on being the top producing office," Ben said.

"Thanks," John replied.

"What's on your mind?"

"Ben, I can't buy your philosophy."

"Why?"

"I built my branch by insuring that the brokers were honest with their clients, revealed all risks, and put them in suitable investments."

"That approach will not last long. Trust me. We used my approach in New York and had phenomenal results."

"This isn't New York, it's Texas. People here resent being deceived. It'll not work here."

"How do you know?"

"Because when I became a broker, we had a manager that adhered to your philosophy. The branch was in shambles."

"What if I told you that you were required to do it or your job is in jeopardy?"

"I would resign."

"You can't afford that."

"I can't afford to do something against my principles."

"John, I want you to think about this. Let's meet again in two days at eight. OK?"

"I'll see you then."

John returned to his branch. He went to his office, checked his messages, and walked to Nick's office.

"How did it go?" Nick asked.

"Not well. He's into the production at all costs and let the client be damned syndrome," John answered.

"That's not good."

"You're right."

"What are you going to do?"

"I don't know yet. I have a meeting with him Wednesday. If he doesn't come off of it, I'm quitting."

"Me too. If you're history, I'm a memory also."

"Don't be hasty. You have a good chance of getting my job. Take it for six months and you'll have good leverage for a manager's job with another firm."

"That makes sense."

John returned to his office. Larry came in.

"What happened?" Larry asked.

John told him. He also stated that he would make a decision after the meeting.

"What are the chances of him letting you run the branch the way you want to?" Larry asked.

"In my opinion, slim and none," John replied.

"If that's true, I'm out of here."

"I can't really blame you. If I can help you in any way, let me know."

"I appreciate that."

On Wednesday, John entered Ben's office.

"What did you decide?" Ben asked.

"I'm not going to compromise my principles. I want you to let me run the branch the way I've been running it."

"I can't do that. If I give you special privileges, it will undermine my credibility with the other managers. You've got to be the dumbest guy I've ever met. I'm showing you a way to increase production and you're rejecting it."

"Your way will not work here. You're the dumb one. In fact, you can take my job and shove it where the sun doesn't shine. I quit."

"You can't do that. I'll give whoever calls a bad reference."

"You've got me mixed up with someone that gives a damn."

"When is you're last day?"

"Today."

"That's wrong. You must give notice."

"I just did."

"Don't you dare return to the branch."

"I'm going there to retrieve my personal effects from my office."

"I'll beat you there and block your entrance."

"Then I'll have to kick your ass all the way to Fort Worth."

John returned to the office and called a brief meeting to say goodbye to his brokers. He also explained to them why he resigned. Then he left. There was much sadness in the office.

John, Terri, and the boys went to Arkansas to look for property. They found two hundred acres between Fort Smith and Hot Springs. The property bordered the Ouachita National Forest. They would have a large roaming area. The forest had an abundance of deer and turkey. In addition, a large clear stream ran through the property. It contained smallmouth bass and other fish species. They would build a house and retire there.